LIAM'S BRIDE

CLAN CONROY BRIDES #1

A CLAN BEAR ROMANCE

EMMA ALISYN

ISBN: 1517331633
First Edition: September 2015

This Book Belongs To:

CONTENTS

CHAPTER

1

Meredith sank to her knees, plunging her hands into moist earth. Closing eyes the same shade as the frothy carrot tops in her basket, she inhaled astringent sunshine and leafy greens. It steadied her, soothed nerves blasted raw by the call from the penitentiary earlier.

"Meredith?"

She pushed aside the Director's pained voice, wet seeping through the knees of her jeans. She didn't care. It anchored her to the present, reminding her why she hadn't left this small town and the troubling memories it held from her childhood. Memories courtesy of the person locked up over one hundred miles away- though not anymore. Her chest squeezed. He wasn't locked up anymore.

"Meredith!"

The snap in Sheane's voice jerked her out of a spiral of panic. Meredith blinked, feeling the blast of afternoon warmth on her cheek, wondered where she'd left her wide brimmed hat. Teenagers laughed several feet away, the tone of one sulky voice warning her she'd have to intervene in a moment or lose an entire crop of carrots. That girl used any weapon at her disposal to defend herself. Even an innocent urban garden.

Meredith looked up. "Sorry, Sheane."

The Director's brow furrowed, thin lines marring the natural beauty of large, loamy eyes. Meredith always thought Sheane belonged somewhere tropical and exotic- somewhere not a small city in Washington, surrounded by apple orchards and coyote and dense stretches of forest preserve.

"I can feel you're... upset, Meredith. But this isn't a problem that can't be solved."

Meredith laughed. One of her after school students glanced over, alerted. She altered the tone of the laugh. Protect the children. They had enough stress in their lives, they didn't need hers. She was sometimes the only island of calm among the adults they dealt with.

"I don't have the *funding* to solve this problem," Meredith replied, fingers twisting viciously in the soil, ripping handfuls of weeds from the roots. "If the new owner plans on converting this place into a culinary school- a *werebear* culinary school, then where does that leave us?" As lunch? She had plenty of meat on her bones.

She surveyed the rows of neatly cultivated plants in various stages of growth, shoulders slumping. Melons ready to pick, seedlings to prepare for the fall garden. Fluffy greens and vines of tomatoes so juicy people traveled from nearby towns to their farmer's market stall just for those, and the relish the kids prepared from the excess fruit.

Sheane sighed. "I understand and I wish there was something more I could do. I've explained to the new owner who the current tenants are, but he's adamant. Maybe you could try talking to him yourself. Your passion is contagious. It might help."

The slump turned to a hunch. Him. Ugh. She didn't want to talk to a *him*. She didn't want to go anywhere near a him who had the money to buy an entire building and convert it into a fancy cooking school. Especially if the him was... a Bear. Werebears were big, growly, and... just big. She'd avoided dealing with a big man since her father had gone to jail. Remembering why he'd gone to jail reinforced the reason she shouldn't have any contact with a werebear.

"I don't think that's a good idea."

Sheane shifted, the abrupt movement signaling her irritation. "Look, Meredith, I understand your issues. Believe me I do. The years I spent working at the women's shelter-"

"I'm nothing like those women," Meredith said, unhunching her shoulders. "I'm not... abused." The yelling, the anger her father inflicted on them during her youth she'd never tolerate from any man. And since most men had temper and ego issues- the bigger the man, the bigger his issues- she avoided them altogether.

Sheane said nothing for a moment. "Meredith..."

"I'll talk to him," she said, wiping the dirt off her hands. Rubbing it off. Dirt was dirt. It had no protective qualities. A movement caught her eye. She glanced past the teenagers, through the rough wood fence and into the parking lot. A car door slammed as a tall man walked away from a slick new SUV. A broad man, even from this distance. Dark hair and stern expression, strides eating pavement as he disappeared from view.

"That's the owner," Sheane said, following Meredith's view.

"It figures." No suit, but all that meant was he made enough money he didn't have to fit himself into an executive image. Kind of like a Mark Cuban.

"Why don't you go talk to him?"

She shook her head. "Not yet. I need time to think about what to say."

"Take time, Meredith," her friend replied, Meredith straining to hear her words. "But not too much time. Sometimes we have to push ourselves, even when we aren't ready. Otherwise you won't grow past your fears."

Meredith excused herself and went inside on the pretext of getting a glass of water. She sat in the worn chair of her tiny office after closing the door and pulling the blinds. The air conditioner worked this year, so the subtle chill iced the stress in her blood right away. Lowering her head onto her arms, she closed her eyes, focusing on her breath.

First problem, the call from her father letting her know the penitentiary released him on parole and he needed a place to stay. The awful frozen panic when she realized he wanted to come stay with her.

Inhale, exhale.

She wasn't a girl any longer, she was a grown woman. A grown woman with a life and friends and teenagers who depended on her. A role in the community. No one remembered whose daughter she was- not to look at her with anger or with pity.

A knock on the door forced her out of her dark reverie. Straightening, she called out. Brick walked in, too slender defiance in cargoes and an oversized flannel shirt. As if she were saying fuck you to the heat. Meredith's eyes zoomed in on her face. Second problem. Pain blossomed on the side of her cheek, vision going dark.

We don't play with Bears, her father roared. *Bear's aren't safe. They aren't human.*

"Mere?"

Meredith forget her problems- shoved them to the back of her mind- rising to walk around her desk. "My God, what happened?"

Brick shrugged, pale eyes flicking over Meredith's shoulders.

"Fight. Just checking in cause I'm late."

Shadows marred the girl's face- bruising inflicted by multiple strikes.

"Do you want to talk to Sheane?"

Brick's lip curled. Meredith sighed. She sympathized. No one liked being labeled a victim- which talking to

Sheane, a former domestic violence counselor, was almost like doing.

"Let's at least go to the kitchen and put ice on it." Meredith pushed with her hand on the door, something occurring to her. "Are you going to get in trouble with your case worker?"

"Only if someone reports it."

Meredith stared at Brick, who stared back, impenetrable as the nick name she'd chosen. Meredith had learned the hard way not to call the girl Rebekah.

"And you don't expect the other person will?"

Brick smirked. Meredith grimaced. "Right. But you can't get into another fight. If you get caught-"

"Yeah, I know. Whatever."

Meredith waffled a minute, then sighed. "Let's go to the kitchen."

"There's people in there, you know."

She opened the door, stepping aside so Brick could precede her. "Oh? Well, we won't be long."

"Dudes. Big dudes."

Oh. Well, that was different. "Huh. Maybe we can-"

She caught the look on the teenager's face before Brick could disguise it under her usual half-bored, half-contemptuous mask.

Okay. Fine.

Meredith turned and marched down the hall, heading to the kitchen with Brick on her heels. They entered, Meredith poking her head in to look both ways. She heard a murmur of voices coming from the direction of the pantry. Good. They were going the opposite direction.

"Come on."

She led the girl to the industrial sized refrigerator, opening the freezer door and grabbing a bag of ice. She rummaged through supplies to find a plastic sandwich bag and measuring cup to scoop the ice- it wouldn't be nice to put bare hands over something others would drink later.

"Here," Meredith said, sealing the baggy and turning towards her student. "Put this on your face." She fixed Brick with a stern look. "Now, tell me what happened. You know you aren't supposed to get into fights, Brick. You could go back to the detention center."

"Only if you tell on me."

Leave it to a teenager to zoom in straight to the point. She knew she was obligated to report the incident, but she couldn't help feeling there was something more to it than Brick would say. Meredith had read the girl's file. The violent incidences in her past were precipitated by someone else attacking her, either physically or verbally. Brick never attacked first. Meredith didn't condone the use of force for verbal assaults- but no one had a right to put their hands on anyone else. Ever. So if the girl was defending herself against real harm, Meredith wasn't going to blame her.

Especially when she wished she'd been strong enough as a child to do the same.

"This is bullshit," Liam said, crumpling the letter in his hand.

Boden grinned at him. "They emailed a copy of the notice, too."

"You agreed to the lottery," Alphonso said, dark eyes calm. He leaned against a shelf, arms folded, long raven braid over a shoulder.

"I didn't think my name would get drawn," Liam growled.

"Stop whining." Boden said. "Find a hot human honey, settle down and have cubs, get hailed as a hero for bringing new genes into the Clan."

"You haven't seen some of the cubs born with the defects," Alphonso said.

Liam looked at him, attention reluctantly caught by the quiet gravity of his friend's voice. His resolve hardened. He'd seen the cubs, had just asked the parents to keep his visits on the down low. The Mother's Circle may have ended the bickering among the Nation about the best course of action to take, but that still didn't mean any perceived show of public support for this new, radical solution wouldn't stick in the jaws of some of the more vocal opponents. And he didn't need to lose precious time spent managing his business by arguing with his Den over his decision.

Too many cubs born in the last several decades with too many genetic defects caused by what boiled down to... inbreeding. Their Nation was small. It was rare to open the Den directory and not be able to find a relative, even a distant one. The best long term solution was to bring fresh genes into each individual Den to strengthen the Clans. Since he was not only Alpha of the local Den, but a member of the family that ruled Clan Conroy, he had a duty to set a good example.

Liam sighed. "What were the goddamn chances? Only ten males per Den drawn from the pool. It was supposed to be a long shot." But he'd promised his mother that if his name was drawn he would comply. Be one of the ten males per Den required to find human mates, the sooner the better.

"Someone's here," Boden said, head turning towards the door. They were closeted in the pantry off the kitchen- mostly because it was stocked, they were hungry and it was as good a place as any to have a quick snack and a quiet conversation since the offices weren't yet cleaned out to prepare for the remodel.

"Relax," Liam said to his younger brother. It wasn't as if they were talking anything top secret, and as soon as werebears started popping up with human mates all over the country, the jig would be up. The occurrence of a Bear-human marriage was rare enough that the media would eventually take notice when there were several. "There are still groups renting space in the building- they have ninety days to vacate."

Boden pushed the door open a sliver, peering out into the kitchen. "Hey, it's women. Cute women."

"I said-"

"I heard you." He left the pantry, moving towards the women.

Liam's fingers itched to settle around his brother's neck. Always distracted by a female. And *human* females at that. He scowled and walked after him. Boden leaned against a counter, body angled towards two women staring at him.

"I'm Boden," his brother was saying. "You ladies must be on staff here."

Liam snorted. He grabbed his brother's shoulder. "Stop harassing the humans and come on."

He stopped speaking, inhaling. An elusive scent of lavender and...

carrots tickled his nose. Beneath it something earthy, tantalizing and quintessentially female. Boden shifted slightly as Liam moved forward, looking down at the female now in his line of vision. He stared, forgetting ire as he met wide eyes the color of chopped herbs. Loose waves of achiote colored hair appeared natural. His fingers twitched. The woman tore her gaze away from his, looking back at Boden, her curvy body stiff as she backed away, grabbing the teenager.

"We were just getting some ice," she said in a low voice. "We'll get out of your way."

Liam stepped forward, Alphonso approaching behind him. "No problem, you weren't disturbing us. What's your name?"

Rosy lips thinning, she refused to look at him. "I'm Meredith. Program director of Teens and Greens."

"Meredith." He stuck out his hand, a silent demand. "I'm Liam. The new owner of this building."

Her shoulders hunched forward, a small tell she controlled instantly, but not before the drapey neck of her pinky tunic flowed around her ample chest, giving him the barest glimpse of smooth flesh. It hugged her body, deceptively modest but accentuating curves before covering her jean clad hips and bottom. The earthy scent sharpened, and Liam realized she was afraid of him. Was it because he was a man, the new owner... or a Bear? Or any combination of the three?

But she took his hand, raising her eyes to his with a suddenness that brought a curve to his lips. She was forcing herself to confront him.

"I know who you are."

She squeezed his hand, strength in the grip. His smile widened. He wasn't

attracted to weak women. Especially
weak human women. But what was he
thinking? His Bear was reacting to her
scent like she was a chunk of dripping
honeycomb. Her attention shifted to the
male behind him. He saw recognition flit
through her eyes, but she addressed
Liam.

"I'd like to talk to you about your
plans for this building," Meredith said,
attempting to pull away. When she
tugged a third time, he let her go.
Slowly. She twitched; he followed her,
shoulders angling so he could lunge
and catch her if she should try and flee
him.

Liam forced his lip, rising in a snarl,
to smooth. Hell. What was wrong with
him? Even Bear females didn't allow the
males to pick them off and walk away
anymore. Well- at least not without the
male guaranteeing her cooperation
beforehand.

He released her and stepped back. Fresh air. Fresh air would help. "Call my office, the receptionist will set up time for you."

Liam made himself turn away, grabbing his brother by the arm and pulling him along. Every step felt as if he were pulling nails from his fingers. Boden watched him, more interested in Liam now than the women.

"I don't believe it," Boden said, expression half speculative, half incredulous.

Liam ignored the two Bears, striding out of the kitchen. They would follow.

"You were damn near quivering when you saw that female. Liam, get her number. Damn, man. Your Bear-"

"Shut up, Boden."

"See?"

Liam saw his brother's smirk out of the corner of his eye, deciding now would be a great time to tackle and pummel him to the ground. It had been a while; Boden was due for some punishment. "Alphonso, tell him."

Alphonso was looking back the way they'd come, eyes narrowed slightly.

"What is it?" Liam asked.

After a moment the male shrugged. "She comes into the bar sometimes- always hanging out with Tamar. That hair is hard to miss."

"I've never seen that color before. It's-" he cut himself off before he said 'beautiful.'

"Guess it won't be so hard for you to get over this prejudice you have against humans," Boden said, smug. "The Mother's will be pleased at how obedient you are."

Liam lunged. He was an Alpha. He was not *obedient,* even if coincidentally, one little human woman made his Bear stand up and roar. Alphonso caught him around the waist.

"The children," the quieter man murmured. They were outside by then, halfway across the lot from where a group of curious teens paused their work in the vegetable and herb garden to watch the men almost fight. Liam had enough time to approve the neatness of the rows and healthy looking plants before shrugging free of his friend.

"I am not prejudiced. I just don't want anything to do with a human female."

"No choice, now."

No, there wasn't was there? But damned if he would admit to Boden that he was right, and after a scent of

Meredith, his fate didn't seem quite so bad anymore.

"What do they feed them?" Brick asked, staring after the three tall, *wide* men as they left the kitchen.

The one whose hand had enveloped Meredith's in an inescapable grip, night sky eyes fixed on her with the pitiless intensity of a carnivorous predator, made her nervous. She'd lost her breath for just a moment, a tingling low in her stomach when he inhaled, nostrils flaring and broad chest widening. She knew about werebears. And she knew Liam was Alpha of the local Den- the collection of closely related families that were a part of a bigger Clan. She'd made it her business to know after- Meredith pulled her mind away from her old guilt.

"They're born big," she said.

Brick glanced at her, alerted by the short tone. "You don't like them cause they're Bears, or cause that's the guy taking the building away from us?"

Meredith frowned. "How did you...?"

The girl snorted. "I have ears."

Sighing, Meredith made another ice baggy to swap when the first melted. The man wasn't what she'd expected. She'd read every newspaper article mentioning him for years, before graduate school and the program forced her to get a life. In her mind the picture of some dismissive executive had formed. Instead, a new age Henry Cavill type in a banded collar shirt, expertly frayed cargoes and leather sandals greeted her, staring at her as if she was lunch. Weren't new agers supposed to be happy pacifists? This male was too... dominant for pacifism, consistent with his Alpha status. The other men would be aggressive, but an Alpha- they were both protective and aggressive and unusually territorial.

"Well, I'll have a talk with him and see if we can stay here."

"I'll do reconnaissance. Don't go in blind."

"Uhh... thanks, but I think I can handle it."

Brick said nothing. Now Meredith had something else to worry about, a teenager already prone to trouble playing detective.

She pressed a hand to her stomach. It still hadn't settled, her mind forcing the image of the dark man behind her eyes, taunting her. Because for the first time in a while, she was attracted to a man. Attracted and afraid, years of her father's teachings she'd worked hard to reverse strumming her nerves. Wonderful. So when she spoke to him again- and from his abrupt withdrawal, she felt convincing him to let her teens stay in the building wouldn't be easy- she'd have to fight nerves, attraction and her instinctive fear of werebears in order to speak coherently. Best thing she could do was start practicing now.

C H A P T E R

2

"Are you sure this is a good idea?" Brick asked. She tugged at the giant pocket on her black cargo skirt. At least it was a skirt.

"It's a great idea," Meredith replied, shoulders squaring as they entered the restaurant.

A blast of cool air and the subtle tinkle of a flute greeted her. Clean, modern decor and people in various styles of dress from business casual to date night sat at dark wood tables bare of linen. Exposed brick studded with bouquets of drying herbs and abstract artwork added to the ambiance.

"Good evening." The hostess greeted them with a smile. Instead of black she wore a loose dress of pale green linen, asymmetrical at the hem to expose wide legged taupe pants and rope sandals. Meredith noticed the mostly female servers dressed similarly, suiting the theme of the restaurant-fresh produce, locally sourced meats, seasonal cuisine. And no menu. Diners ate what the chef presented. And the chef was notorious for presenting interesting things. Meredith knew because when she'd Googled the new owner of the YWCA, Liam Conroy, his whole history as a trained chef and restaurateur flooded the results.

She'd cursed herself, wondering why she hadn't recognized him and his name beforehand. A *Conroy*, the werebear family whose past intimately entangled with the ragged remains of her own family. She'd almost given up right then- but he couldn't know who she was, not with her common last name, if he'd even bothered to look at her paperwork. And there were the kids who depended on her to keep the program alive- it was the only safe place some of them had to go.

"We have a reservation," Meredith informed the hostess.

"Of course. Please follow me."

They sat at a small two person table in front of the main window, giving them a charming view of early evening foot traffic as well as the patrons of the restaurant. A server brought wine and freshly squeezed juice for Brick, and soon an amuse-bouche was placed in front of them; a tiny squash blossom stuffed with a decadently creamy filling of savory cheese and mushroom, lightly fried.

"So how are you going to get his attention?" Brick asked when they were on their first course, a gazpacho with southwestern flavors and slivers of bright avocado on top.

Meredith smiled grimly, enjoying the soup. "I'm going to send back a dish." Which from the various blogs and Yelp reviews was certain to gain her an in person response.

"He's kinda an ass for not returning your appointment request. Are you sure you don't want to just skip out on the bill?"

Meredith leveled the teen with a *look.* Brick grinned, unrepentant.

"How is the new placement going?" Meredith asked, changing the subject. Since she'd known Rebekah, the girl had been in two different foster homes. The first time, the family moved out of state and the second time the mother had her fourth baby and decided Brick's purpose in life was to be used as free child care. While Meredith sympathized with trying to handle four children and a foster teen all at once- Brick wasn't supposed to be a live-in nanny.

The girl's expression darkened, closing down in a snap. "It's going."

Alarm bells jingled. "Do you want to talk about it?" she asked gently.

"No."

"Alright. You know you can if you ever need to." She changed the subject, heading off gathering clouds. Building trust required patience. "We should take pictures of the food- the others will want to see."

The meal was delicious, but during the final course Meredith steeled her spine, waving over the server.

"I'm sorry, can you return this dessert to the kitchen?"

The server looked nonplussed. "Of course. May I ask..."

Meredith plowed ahead, raising her chin. "The berries are bland, the whipped cream watery and the sponge sickly sweet. It's just not to my taste."

The server's eyes darted towards the kitchen. "Of course. I'll... let Chef know."

That was what she was counting on.

"She said *what?*" Liam ignored the server's flinch, slapping a towel on the counter. "Take the pass," he snapped at his sister, also his sous chef.

"Don't kill the customers," Norelle murmured, flipping her fish as he stalked into the dining room.

Damned if he'd let the swine who insulted his food live. Bland? Watery? *Sickly?* It was untenable.

The server scuttled along half way to the table and then changed her mind, abandoning Liam's warpath before he placed himself in front of.... he recognized the flame red hair of the woman with her back to him before he recognized the black lipped and heavily lined eyes of the teenager staring at him sideways. The same teen he'd seen in his building a week ago.

Meredith- he hadn't forgotten her name- turned her head, and he forgot about the teenager.

"Chef."

He stared down at her, controlling a desire to march back into the kitchen and personally make her a new dessert- it would piss off the pastry chef- struggling to hold onto his legendary temper. Her husky tone and uncertain but brave eyes guttered his artists' indignation.

"You didn't enjoy the dish?" he asked, voice pitched for her ears alone.

He observed the tinge of pink along her cheeks with interest. When was the last time he'd seen a female over the age of thirteen blush? She cleared her throat as his eyes traveled down the pale column to her chest, clad in another drapey thingy, this time a soft peach that brought out the rose tone of her skin. Short, pearlescent nails tapped the water glass at her plate, then stilled.

"No, the dessert was lovely."

Liam's brows drew together. "Then-"

"I wanted to talk to you. You've been avoiding my appointment request."

Mossy eyes speared him, wide and clear, demanding an answer.

Liam folded his arms. "I've been busy." He cut himself off, scowling. Was he really giving her an explanation? He didn't have to give her an explanation.

She lowered her eyes. The hand fiddling with the wineglass curled into a ball. She placed it in her lap, a vulnerable gesture.

"I haven't been avoiding you," he said, sighing, arms unfolding. He would have met temper for temper, but this quiet, hesitant dignity undid him. A brash woman he would have dismissed instantly. "Why don't we talk now?"

She looked up quickly, eyes widening as he gestured. The hostess brought him a chair, plucking it from one of the few empty tables. He turned it around with a nod of thanks, folding his arms across the back.

"Now." He gave her his full attention. "Here I am. Talk."

Her lips rubbed together. He forced his face to remain neutral, masking his reaction. He wondered how her face would look flushed with passion, green eyes glittering with the fire of jewels as she moaned beneath him. If she were his, he'd drape her neck in ropes of polished jade and amber beads. Long ropes nestled between the valley of her breasts- Liam jerked his mind away from the image, thighs bunching as his body approved his thoughts. Thankful he wore his chef's coat loose rather than fitted.

He inhaled, filling his lungs with the scent he remembered, this time overlaid with the familiar aromas of his food and kitchen. The combination stirred something inside him deeper than the mere physical. She felt both exotic and familiar- as if she belonged. To him, to his home.

"I'd like you to consider renewing our lease," she said. Her voice started with the faintest tremble, then steadied. He approved of her courage. It wasn't easy facing down a Bear, and especially not an Alpha. Though human, she would still be subconsciously affected by his dominance and have a hard time making demands of him. She wouldn't quite understand why- but if she were weak she would agree to anything he asked if he weren't careful.

"You're aware I'm converting the building into a culinary school with a television studio?" he asked. She nodded. "Our plans require every bit of space there is."

"I understand, but I think Teens and Greens offers value to what you're trying to do."

"Oh?" His raised brow invited explanation.

She tucked loose hair behind her ear. His eyes followed the gesture, wanting to wrap the strand around his hand, use it as a rope to bind her to him for a kiss. "We teach teenagers urban gardening. Your restaurant sources its ingredients from local farmers. What if your school included a teaching garden as well? I'm a licensed instructor- I'd be happy to provide instruction and space for your students to grow their own herbs."

The idea interested him. Though he hadn't initially considered it, focused on the culinary side of his business, it made sense. He said nothing though, waiting.

She hurried to fill the silence. "And of course, my services would be offered as part of the lease. It wouldn't be any bother to include additional students. It's more help to keep the garden. And I was considering expanding to a nearby lot as well next year. It would be good publicity for your school."

Hmm. The kind of feel good hometown publicity that would get him in the newspaper. Maybe even a television special he could pitch to a big name network along with what he already had planned.

Liam stood. "I'll think about it and contact you."

Her chin lifted. "Soon. If the answer is no then I'll have to make other plans." Her voice trembled on the word 'no.' He wondered what her other plans would be if his response wasn't to her liking.

"I'll contact you."

"I have something to say," the teenager interjected. He met her eyes. A less secure adult might meet the challenge in her face with aggression. Even now Meredith was waving at the girl to hush, forehead furrowed.

He lifted a hand, taking his seat. One didn't injure a child covered in bruises to teach a lesson. "It's alright. Go ahead, daughter."

Meredith opened her mouth, then subsided, stifling a sigh. "Go ahead, Brick."

"The garden is important."

He waited for the girl to gather her thoughts. She held up under his regard- impressive.

"Some of us don't have any... cool places to hang out. And we can take the vegetables to our families, and it helps out sometimes. I don't think it's fair to take it away because you want to be rich and teach rich people to make useless food."

Liam waited a beat. "Are you finished?" He understood the sentiment, though her worldview required adjustment if she considered culinary students 'rich people', but she needed to be taught to communicate without anger.

She nodded, a jerk of the head, and he rose again, staring down at her gravely.

"Thank you for your insight," he said. "Please believe me, I'll consider everything that's been asked of me. I won't make a hasty decision. Okay?"

The women nodded, and he could sense some of the tension leave the girl. He turned to go when she said, "The food was good. I haven't had anything like it before."

Liam paused, turned back, then held out his hand. She shook it, surprised.

"That, young lady, is a wonderful compliment. Bring a friend by for lunch one day- on me."

The girl grinned. "Cool, man. I mean, Chef. Thanks."

He inclined his head, meeting Meredith's wide, glimmering eyes. She held herself still, looking down as soon as realization they were staring lit her eyes. Liam left them, forcing himself to turn and walk away. Something in him wanted to remain in her presence, wanted to reassure her that she would have her lease and her garden and whatever else she needed to make her program a success. His desire to please her puzzled and disturbed him. She was human, and he was reacting as if- Liam cut the thought off. The best thing he could do was clear his nostrils with the aromas of cooking food.

But it took a long time.

Meredith let out a shaky breath. She concentrated on relaxing her jaw, one tooth at a time. "That went okay."

More than okay. He'd listened with every indication of seriousness. And the kindness he'd shown Brick-Meredith's heart softened. Men like that made good fathers, good husbands. It was too bad men like that were rare.

"He didn't say 'hell no' or kick us out, so I guess."

She half grimaced, half sighed and raised a hand to signal for the check. Lowered it back to her lap to hide the fine trembles. It had taken everything to remain composed in his presence. The warmth, the command he projected affected her, as if the air was super charged with pheromones. The server came to her table, smiles and graciousness.

"Your meal is compliments of the Chef, ma'am."

"Double cool," Brick said.

Meredith stared at the server, pride battling with practicality. The reality of her dwindling program budget and narrow personal finances swayed her towards practicality. "Oh. Well- give him my thanks and compliments for a fabulous meal. I'll leave a positive review," she added.

The server smiled again. "We appreciate it. Honest reviews are the lifeblood of every small business."

"He's kinda nice, you know?" Brick said as they left. "Maybe he likes you. I thought he was checking you out a little hard, but I figured it was a werebear thing. They're supposed to be intense."

She felt as if she'd faced a firing squad, only it was a squad of one and she was naked, bared to the heated gaze of a male whose gun wasn't the steel type. She felt fire in her cheeks and bit her lip to distract herself. There was no denying she... reacted to him. But it absolutely wasn't attraction. Just nervousness, and the knowledge of who he was. Whose son he was. Meredith paused at the crosswalk, closing her eyes briefly. If he ever found out about her father, he would never renew the lease. The smart thing to do would be to get at least a three year contract out of him- just in case. And then see as little of him as possible.

"I think it's just a chef thing," Meredith said, opening her eyes as she heard Brick moving. They'd taken a bus to avoid expensive downtown parking. The meal counted as an expense of the program, but that wasn't necessary now.

She wondered if he would call her, or if the free meal was a parting gesture of sympathy to ease his conscience.

CHAPTER

3

They rode the bus to the YWCA, Meredith driving Brick the rest of the way to her foster home. She hadn't met the family- somehow the teen always avoided introducing her. Meredith worried about the placement, but also knew from nearly two years experience she wouldn't get a word out of the girl unless Brick wanted to talk.

Thinking of family, on a whim Meredith drove to the diner managed by her mother. Kathy would be on duty; Friday evenings were busy shifts. If it was hectic enough, her mother would rope Meredith into waiting tables for tips only, since she wasn't officially an employee and on the payroll.

Meredith had moonlighted on more Fridays than she could count. Teaching jobs were hard to come by in a small town, and though she scraped by conducting adult ESL classes online during the day, money was tight. Another frustration. It seemed in every aspect of her life money was an issue. And then someone like Liam Conroy waltzed in and just bought a whole building as if it money was no object.

Resentment welled up, followed by guilt. That man and his family deserved whatever good fortune came their way. She had no right to feel jealousy at his success.

"Mere!"

Her mother spotted her as soon as she walked in the door, noise blasting Meredith's ears; the din of chatter, dishes clinking, cooks hawking orders, and high energy music a cacophony in the background. A marked difference from the restaurant she'd just left. It felt like home.

"Hey, Ma. Need help?"

Kathy shoved an apron at her. "Take section three. Cory called in with a sick kid. Emergency room."

Meredith grimaced in sympathy. Double whammy. A hospital co-pay and loss of what could be upwards to two hundred dollars in tips on a six hour shift. It was one of the many reasons why she'd always been careful with birth control- outside of marriage, how could she afford to take care of a child? So she directed her maternal instincts into caring for the teenagers in her program, and maybe one day...

She waited tables for two solid hours before a lull in customers allowed her to take a quick break. Leaning against a stack of boxes containing dry supplies in the employee break room—more of a storage closet with a couple of card tables set aside, her mother joined her a few minutes later, sighing as she kicked off her black restaurant shoes.

"This is the first break I've had in six hours," Kathy said, rubbing her feet. "Paydays are always like this."

"We've both earned a slice of pie after shift."

"With double ice cream." Mother grinned, abandoning feet to rebraid her dusty red hair. "Did you come to work or hang out?"

Meredith sighed, staring at the table, fingers tapping the hard plastic. "Ma..."

"Uh-oh. What's wrong?"

There was no way to say it, except to say it. "The YWCA is being sold to the son of Gerald Conroy."

Mother's entire countenance changed from a happy though exhausted woman, to someone tense from instant negative stress.

"That's not good," Kathy replied, voice quiet. "You have to move the program to another location?"

"There *is* no other location. I... asked him to let us stay."

Grey eyes widened. "Meredith, does he know who your father is?"

"No."

Kathy shook her head. "There is no scenario where withholding that information will work out well."

"I was going to ask for a three year contract."

"*Meredith*. You have to tell him."

"He-"

"He's not a bad boy." She began tapping the table in time with Meredith, stopped, lowered her hands to her lap. "What your father did is not your fault. You need to be honest, Meredith."

Honesty wasn't always what it was cracked up to be. What she *needed* was an affordable space for her program. What she *needed* was to not have to uproot an entire garden right before fall. What she *needed* was some kind of luck in her life instead of everything being complicated, for once.

"I'll think about it. When I talked to him he seemed..." she hesitated, trying to put into words an impression of him she didn't quite yet understand. His body language, which coming from any other man would have led her to think- but that was ridiculous.

"Yes?"

"He didn't say no," she said after a minute, blushing. Kathy's eyes narrowed.

Meredith stood, hurriedly. "That's my break. I'll do another two hours and then head out, alright?"

"Huh. Meredith Lizanne-

"See ya, Ma."

She went back to her tables, avoiding the suspicion in her mother's eyes, cursing her pale skin. She couldn't help it. When she thought about the way he looked at her with such focus-all she could picture in her mind was how he would look above her. Inside her. It wasn't until she was on her way home that she realized she'd completely forgotten to tell her mother that her father had called from jail, and would soon be out on parole.

She spent the next evening at her best friend's house, going over the events of the previous week. It occurred to Meredith that since Tamar's boss was the man she'd seen in Liam's company- Alphonso- Tamar might have some insight.

"You did what?" Tamar's shriek nearly drowned out her infant's squeal as her tiny foot hit a plush bear swinging over her.

Meredith slanted her a *look*, irritated. "I think I was creative."

Tamar stared at her, deep russet eyes wide. "You're crazy. He's a Bear. Do you know how territorial they get? One day this jerk insulted Al's choice in new upholstery for the booths, and Al growled at him and threw him out of the bar. Literally threw him. The police just said they couldn't help suicide by Bear."

Meredith sighed, defeated. "It seemed like a good idea at the time. He was real nice about it. Comped the meal and invited Brick back for free."

"Brick? That smart-mouthed, Goth faced-"

"Don't talk about her like that. She's a kid who's had a tough life. She's been working on her attitude."

Tamar shut up. "Okay, that was mean."

"Besides," Meredith continued, "she didn't have a dad growing up and her mother-"

The single mom held up a hand, full lips tight. "I get it."

They both glanced at the baby squirming on the activity rug in front of them. One of her hands caught a plastic rattle, and she couldn't quite figure out how to disengage. Luminous black eyes and curly hair, golden brown skin a cross between her mother's deep hued tone and the Caucasian father Meredith only knew as the White Guy Who Knocked Tamar Up, the baby was the most beautiful Meredith had ever seen.

"It's not your fault-" Meredith began.

Tamar smiled, nothing happy in the expression. "How is it not my fault? No one made me have unprotected sex with a- with her father."

"Have you tried contacting him again?"

The silence was reply enough. "He knows where I am," Tamar said. "If he wanted to see me, he could get on his damn motorcycle and be here in five minutes."

"Um... motorcycle? You didn't mention he had a motorcycle." Meredith's eyes narrowed. "Wait a minute. You told me he was from here originally. There aren't that many guys from here who own motorcycles."

Tamar avoided looking at her. "Just forget about it, okay? Forget I said anything."

That wasn't likely, but she could set it aside for now, like she'd set it aside for the last year. Meredith didn't know the whole story of this guy and Tamar, but she thought her friend was being too quick to accept his non-involvement.

She shrugged. "Anyway, Liam said he'd consider it. He seemed interested."

"Liam Conroy is never interested in anything a human has to say."

Meredith winced. "My Dad is to blame for that. Liam can't ever find out."

Tamar rolled her eyes. She'd worn mascara today, living on the edge. Meredith knew Tamar's Pastor father forbade his daughters wearing makeup. "Melodrama. Worst case scenario is he does, and you just have to find somewhere else to park your program. Better get a backup plan together, girl."

"I'm working on it." Only she wasn't. The Y was her second home, and she wanted to stay. She'd just have to convince Liam to let her.

Liam felt eyes on him from across the street. Continuing to work, he waited. She'd come to him when she was ready. This early in the morning on a Saturday, the sun was already warm and a considerate breeze provided a bit of relief. The porch he'd rebuilt had finished drying weeks ago, but he hadn't gotten around to coating it with another layer of white paint until today. The first day he'd taken off since he could remember.

Finally she approached, emerging from the cover of trees. His house sat on the edge of a section of forest reserve specially cordoned off for Bear use, no humans allowed. The humans might resent it, but the fact was his people had been in North America for hundreds of years before the pilgrims ever landed. When the first Europeans had tried to conquer Bear inhabited lands, they'd been met with bloody resistance. Over the years, sheer numbers of humans and sheer bloody aggression from Bears produced a stalemate; so now the Bears owned entire vast tracks of forest land reserved for their use. It wasn't like the old days, but it was... something. And since his family, the Conroy's- a name adopted generations ago- controlled this area of the state, he was charged as the local Den Alpha with maintaining their borders, and their relationship with local humans.

"Hello, Mother."

She studied him, eyes inscrutable. The sun brightened the burnt caramel color, a shade of brown no human possessed. He glanced at her face, paused, and drew himself up to his full height. He'd need every inch he could get; right now she was an Elder

addressing an Alpha, and not his
mother.

"I spoke with your sister,"
Gwenafar said.

"Yeah? She talks too much."

Liam knew he may have
mentioned Meredith, may have been...
frustrated in some of his word choices.
The evening before, after the human
woman left his restaurant, it had taken
him until after closing to recover from
the encounter. Not recover- that wasn't
quite the right word. But... return to
equilibrium. She'd put him off balance.
His desire to please her, his desire to
take her home and chain her to his
bed, disturbed him. He couldn't recall
reacting so strongly to a female before,
Bear or human. Certainly not human.
Norelle had nearly chewed his head off
because of his snappish distraction.

"It seems as if you've taken the Circle's edict seriously," his mother said. "I was prepared for more… pushback."

He scowled. He was no tame Alpha. "I've given the Circle's edict all the consideration it deserves."

She sat down on one of the dry steps, patting the spot next to her. He sat next to her reluctantly, but he couldn't disrespect his mother.

"You don't agree with it? The doctors we spoke with were convincing."

It wasn't that he didn't agree. He'd read the reports along with all the other Alphas. "You know how I feel about humans," he replied.

"Yes, I know, and I think it's a shame you allow one bad seed to cloud your judgment of an entire species."

She called the man who'd shot his father a 'bad seed?' That scum was a bit worse than bad seed. And if Liam ever saw that man in this town, or any of that man's sons- if he had any- then he'd make it his duty to see they paid for the sins of the father.

"Is it so wrong to want to stay with our own kind?"

"No, not wrong. But we need the Alphas to set a good example. If we don't introduce fresh genes into our community, we will die out."

He understood that. But he thought seeking human brides should be a last resort. There were werebears in the international community they could find mates among. Granted, the politics of that would be... convoluted. And some of the European Bear cultures were a bit weird. But it could be done.

"I'll do my duty, mother," he said, an edge in his tone.

She sighed. "Tell me about this woman your sister said you met."

He shrugged, staring up at the sky. "She runs a program at the YWCA. Gardening for problem kids."

"Oh? That sounds promising if she works with children. Is she pretty?"

Pretty? She was fucking hot. Lush curves and fiery hair. And an attitude under the shyness that turned him on.

"She's not ugly."

Gwenafar laughed, wincing at the same time. "I hope you have a bit more finesse when trying to woo her."

Finesse? He wanted to just toss her over his shoulder and have done with it. But he supposed things weren't done like that anymore. Especially not with delicate human women. A Bear female would assume that if he staked a claim, his intentions were good. If she allowed him to carry her off, it was tantamount to a commitment. But then, he wouldn't be carrying off a Bear female unless he was ready to mate her anyway. So was he really prepared to mate this woman? Marry her? His instincts seemed to be pushing him in that direction. Damnit.

"I see you have some thinking to do." His mother stood. "I'll leave you to your busy work. Just remember- this woman isn't to blame for the bad things in our past, Liam. Don't take your pain and anger out on her."

He kissed her on the cheek before she left. It wasn't a long walk back to her house- his childhood home.

His family allowed him another generous thirty minutes of work time before the next volley. Boden bounded up the steps, appearing from the side of the house. He liked to jump fences between yards and cross the alley rather than take the time to walk around the entire block. Lazy. Liam wondered what Meredith would think of the werebear family tendency to live in the same neighborhoods their entire lives. Entire extended families staying within walking distance of each other. It was rare for a member of a Den to leave his or her place of birth and rearing. Which was the problem.

"Did Ma stay long?"

His brother could scent that their mother had been by, but he wouldn't know for how long. "Yes, she did. Were you sent to do your part to talk me into this mating?"

"Bit soon, isn't it?" Boden disappeared in the house, came back out a moment later with two cold beers. "I know we need brides, but you just met a girl. No one said you had to rush things. Though, if you aren't interested, let me know. I think I'd like a stab at her." Boden grinned. "Literally."

Liam growled, the involuntary rumble tearing from deep in his chest and startling them both. Boden held up his hands, one clutching the sweating can. "Hey, no foul. Clear field, bro. Just let me know if you decide to step back."

"She's mine."

Boden saluted him with the can. "You should probably tell her that, then. Humans don't do the whole mate on first sniff thing."

Liam turned on his heels, storming into the house. The floorboards creaked. They were refinished, carefully buffed into gleaming warm life, but the original wood still creaked. Especially under his weight. A few colorful woven rugs were scattered in each room, absorbing some of the shock.

He entered his state of the art kitchen where he kept the house phone. He was old fashioned like that- he still believed in having an actual home phone number. Liam snatched it up from the black base, opening a drawer to withdraw a small notepad. He'd already talked the YWCA director into giving him Meredith's phone number- just in case he needed to reach her for business purposes over the weekend.

Dialing, broad knuckles rapping against the granite counter.

"Hello?"

"Meredith." He managed, barely, to rein in the snap of his voice.

"Mr. Conroy?"

He gritted his teeth. "Liam. Look, I want to talk to you about your proposal."

"Okay," she said slowly. "I'll be in the office Monday at the usual time."

"No. I want to see you tonight."

"Mr.-Liam- I don't think-"

"Don't think. I'll be at the Y at 9pm. Meet me in the kitchen."

He hung up before she could say anything else, mind skipping ahead in the day. Plotting, planning. Deciding on how best to seduce one half shy, half suspicious human woman. And making it seem like it was all her idea.

CHAPTER
4

Meredith wasn't sure if Liam's call was a good sign, or an ominous one.

Granted, she didn't really know him... but he had sounded strange. Brusque and strained at the same time. She wondered if it was safe to meet him alone at night, and debated leaving a message for her mother.

But despite her unease over the apparent quickness of his decision- she assumed that's why he wanted to meet- she didn't feel as if Liam were dangerous. At least, not *dangerous* dangerous. Whether or not he threatened her as a woman remained to be seen. She would have to be on her guard, hide her reluctant attraction and remain focused on business. Make sure her heart and body stayed out of his reach.

Her yellow Dotson coughed into the parking lot five minutes before their meeting time. The only other vehicle present was the slick SUV she'd noticed the other day.

After unlocking the building's side door and walking through the halls, she stuffed her hands into her jeans to hide the slight tremble in her fingers. She supposed she could blame it on her morning coffee. Being caffeine sensitive, if she drank more than a cup her body would go haywire. But she'd poured more milk into the mug than coffee, so knew she couldn't make that excuse.

Shouldering the double doors of the commercial kitchen open, Meredith stopped short. The sizzle and scent of meat and spices seduced her nose. She inhaled, stomach rising to attention and wagging its tail. Food. Real food, not the single gal meals she threw together when fresh produce was scarce. Liam turned slightly, intense eyes spearing her with a brief look.

"Sit down," he said, indicating a table with his chin. She followed the motion, noticing he'd taken a table from the attached break room and placed it along a wall, covered in a white cloth and set with fresh wildflowers.

"Chef's table," she said without thinking, staring. Bear and whimsical didn't seem to go together. It put her at ease- a little.

A rumble of agreement came from his chest. "Go. Sit."

She obeyed automatically, caught by the authority in his tone, walking towards the table and taking a seat before she remembered she had promised to remain... professional.

Surveying the table, eyebrows knit, she wondered if *he* was trying to keep it professional. It didn't look like it. Maybe she hadn't imagined the zing of something between them. Though she was inexperienced with men- by choice her relationships remained few- she wasn't stupid. She could read basic body language.

And a man who wasn't interested in a woman didn't cook her dinner. Not when he already had the upper hand.

Meredith decided bluntness to be the best weapon. "I'm a little confused."

Dishes clinked. A moment later he approached with white restaurant plates, sliced meat delicately arranged over creamy potatoes, topped with a bed of fluffy fresh micro-greens. A red sauce swirled around the entire dish. He placed the plates on the table, disappeared into the walk-in and returned a moment later with chilled glasses and wine.

He sat, pouring ruby liquid into glasses. She couldn't read his expression so instead watched fingers graceful despite their size move with a chef's deftness. He placed the glass in front of her, waited until she took a sip.

"Do you like it?"

"I'm not much of a wine person, but it has a bit of sweetness to it."

He nodded, gesturing at her plate. "I thought a talk over a meal would be enjoyable and I wanted to get the lay of the kitchen before I finalize designs for the remodel. Seemed a shame to waste the food."

"You have to cook in it first to get a feel for it?" Meredith asked, taking a guess. Relaxing now that she knew the setup wasn't *about* her, but more a gracious inclusion *of* her. She sliced into the meat, the knife moving through with such ease she set it aside. Beef melting in her mouth, her eyelids drooped. "Oooooh. This is good."

"Hmm. It's not too bland?"

Eyes reopening, she felt another blasted blush. "I'm sorry. The food at your restaurant really was very good. I was just trying to get your attention."

"You got it," he replied, voice dry, dark eyes glinting. They caught her for a moment, capturing her attention to the point she realized the purity of black surrounding his pupils was absolute. Not a fleck of brown, striation of russet. No lessening of the bottomless coal darkness.

"These potatoes taste different," she said, voice pitched high.

"Not potatoes. Cauliflower and leek."

"Much healthier," she said, managing to level her tone. Heat faded to friendly warmth under her nervous regard, his lashes suddenly lowering to allow her to break the stare. She cleared her throat. "You know my teens grow both of those in the garden. We had plans next season to become certified as organic. I had them studying natural pest prevention methods this year, and we sourced our seeds from local organic farmers."

He took a sip of his wine. She watched his throat move, helpless to look away even when a small smile curve his lips.

"I thought about what you said." He reached across the table, a finger trailing along the bone of her cheek. She didn't move, the skin under his touch hyper aware. "A garden attached to the school that produces for the restaurant *is* a smart business move. I hadn't really considered it because I don't have time to manage it."

"Now you do." She smiled brightly, sitting back in her chair. "We'll do it for you and think of all the new customers you'll get. The students' families would be happy to go to the restaurant that features produce they've grown."

"Yes." His hand lowered to the table, fingers curling, expression impassive. "I can see the benefits on several angles. So I'm going to renew your lease at the same rate."

Her breath caught. She opened her mouth to thank him, but he shook his head, forestalling her. "Don't thank me yet. I want something more."

Liam's voice caressed the word more. She suppressed a shiver. He didn't say anything for several moments, watching her face. Meredith's eyes narrowed with impatience. "Yes?"

"I know you have an M.Ed."

What she had was an M.Ed's worth of student loan debt the government considered her too poor to pay. She could always move to a bigger city and get a teaching job, but she didn't want to leave her teenagers. *They* were her students, even if the classroom wasn't a recognized one.

"I'd like you to co-teach a class with me. Arrange the curriculum."

"What?" Meredith stared at him, beyond surprised. They'd gone from her possibly facilitating some informal instruction in sustainable gardening, to teaching an actual class.

"That's possible, of course," she began. "But I have to work-"

He waved a hand. "I'd pay you. I'm not trying to get anything for free." His expression darkened, stare intensifying, seizing her lungs and limbs in momentary stasis. "Women are *never* free. Especially the ones worth... buying."

There was something inherently insulting about that statement, but she was having trouble thinking past his focused regard. Meredith forked food into her mouth in an attempt to put some distance between them.

"It occurred to me that any chef worth his or her salt should know how to grow their own food," he continued softly. "I have a small kitchen garden at my home. I think it best if we meet there to arrange how the lessons will go. And I'd like some... privacy... to see what you know."

"I prefer to work here," she replied, setting the fork down. "The garden is much more extensive and it's the environment the students will be learning in, after all."

Liam smiled. It wasn't anywhere near friendly, but it *was* predatory. "No. My building, my school, my students- my way."

Meredith's lips pursed. "I'll *think* about it." She stood, stiffly. She couldn't take it anymore, her body's relentless clamoring. Her thighs clenched. "Thank you for the meal."

Liam rose after her, slowly, drawing up to his full height. He lifted a hand, fingertip outlining the shape of her lips, a feather light touch that shouldn't have felt erotic, but interrupted her breathing. The brush of his finger seared her face. She took a small step back, a tiny flinch she immediately regretted.

"You don't have much choice, Meredith. None, in fact."

"What is it you really want?" she asked. He wasn't acting like a business owner speaking to a potential employee. Tension arched between them. He stepped forward, his body not quite touching hers.

"I think you have an idea, Meredith." He paused. "I'm willing to give you time to get used to it."

Of all the arrogant, vague, tantalizing, unromantic but intriguing... offers. Meredith couldn't deny her own attraction, the spark between them.

"You're a Bear. I'm not."

"I don't care. Besides, my Bear wanted you first. I'm... following along."

Her eyes narrowed. "Is this where you tell me you're attracted to me in spite of yourself, Mr. Conroy?"

He laughed. "Houston, right? That man was a moron."

She crossed her arms over her full chest. "Austen, not Houston, was a woman, and the *author*."

Liam shrugged. "Whatever. Human books." His dark brow rose, eyes glimmering, steady on hers. "Are you going to cooperate, Meredith? Or do we do this dance the difficult way?"

She inhaled, let her breath out in a rush. "I- we can't. I'm not looking for a relationship right now." Especially not with a Conroy. *Especially* not with her father coming out of jail soon. Meredith paled, thoughts jarring her back into the reality of her situation with Liam. He could *never* find out who she was. He would tear the lease up instantly, leaving her teenagers in the lurch. Not to mention the threat to her heart if her emotions followed where her body was leading.

"What's wrong?" he asked softly. "You look like you're in pain."

"I- thank you for dinner. I have to go."

"Meredith-"

She whirled, agitated, heading towards the double doors. "I have to go!"

It took three steps before he lifted her off her feet, halting her rush to get away. Meredith felt the heat of his torso against her back as he hauled her against him, arms wrapped around her. He bent slightly, so much taller than her.

"Don't run from me, Meredith," he snapped, voice edged. "It... activates certain responses you aren't ready to deal with."

"You don't know me," she said, forcing the tremble out of her voice. She'd embarrassed herself with a mildly hysterical retreat, she wouldn't compound it by saying or acting in any other way that was less than dignified. Damnit. "And physical attraction isn't enough for a relationship."

He laughed silently. She felt the movement of his chest, an unvoiced rumbled. "I think it's interesting we went from co-teachers to being in a relationship."

Meredith cringed in embarrassment, before anger took over. He was playing games. Meredith twisted in his arms, hands pushing against the rock wall of his chest. He looked at her, a small grin on his mouth.

Teasing, for the most part, but with an edge.

"Sweetheart, you aren't going anywhere unless I let you, so you might as well talk."

"You're playing games, not talking," she said hotly, forgetting shyness, forgetting he was a big man and it was probably safer not to challenge his temper. "You know damn well you've implied you want more than a professional interaction from me. I'm not misreading signals."

The grin softened into a smile. "Don't be mad, I'm teasing you, Meredith." He hesitated. "The truth is, I didn't expect what I'm feeling. When the Bear shows such interest, it's hard to resist. We've learned, over the years, not to."

"I thought werebears mated for life? I didn't know they did short term, casual things."

His lips quirked again. Meredith held his eyes a long moment, waiting for a response, before it dawned on her the silence *was* his response.

"You mean..." she knew something about werebears. She'd made it her business to know at least something. But Liam couldn't mean what he was allowing her, by his silence, to think. His head dipped.

"Yes, I'm thinking things are heading somewhere more permanent than 'casual,' sweetheart. But I'm willing to take it slow."

He released her then, almost reluctantly. "But, just so you don't get any ideas about *how* slow..."

Meredith braced herself, feeling his intent before his head and shoulders swooped down, lips capturing hers in a deceptively soft kiss. He didn't touch her except for his mouth on hers, giving her the choice of whether to accept or pull away.

She couldn't have pulled away after the first brush of satiny skin. His mouth tasted of wine, breath an elusive aroma of male, forest and herbs. And despite the softness, she felt steel underneath, a determination to prove she was becoming as hopelessly entangled as he. Because if his Bear really was urging him towards her, Meredith knew he had no real choice in the matter. He could fight fate and be miserable, or make the best of it.

His tongue invaded her mouth, the touch of him sending a pulse of fire straight to her clit, tightening her belly and sending tingles down her spine. And then she couldn't think, couldn't analyze anymore. Could only feel, could only yearn for him to step into her body so she could rub herself against him. Her hands rose, clenching air, seeking flesh. In that moment he stepped back, eyes hot with satisfaction, skin drawn taunt over the slashing bones of his face.

"Think about it, but not for long," he repeated. "I'll be waiting for you."

CHAPTER

5

Sundays she slept in, went over garden plans for the following week and covered shifts at the diner. In the evenings she subbed for teachers taking a last minute break.

This morning she woke early to pounding on her front door. The apartment wasn't enclosed; anyone could walk up to her front door similar to a motel.

Meredith scrambled, halting a fall from bed just as her mind awoke. Who would knock on her door on a Sunday morning? Most of her college friends lived out of town. Meredith was the last hold over from their small town upbringing. Except Tamar- but then she had moved away, too, and only come back to raise her baby somewhere quiet.

She pulled sweats on underneath her oversized sleep shirt, tugging her hair into a quick sloppy-neat pony tail. Thank God the just woke up look was a recognized style. Peering through the peephole, her heart stopped.

"I know you're there, Mere," her father Harvey said in a scratchy voice. Paused and cleared his throat. "I heard the footsteps."

She leaned her forehead against the door, heart thumping. How the hell could she have forgotten? Her father. Knees feeling weak, Meredith's mind raced. How could she open the door? How couldn't she?

"Let's just talk, sweetheart, and then I'll go away if you want."

Her father calling her 'sweetheart' jarred Meredith, twisting the muscles of her stomach. Her mind recalled the image of the man whose use of the same endearment sparked a completely different response in her. A warm response, where with her father she only felt dread.

Meredith looked through the peephole again, this time studying the man she hadn't seen in years. He looked thin, graying brown hair shaggy, a stubble on his cheeks and chin. Faded jeans and a plain t-shirt added to the hitchhiker look he sported with the army green satchel slung over his shoulders. His hunched, slumped posture shrunk his size. This wasn't the big, stressed and mostly angry man she remembered.

With a small shock, she realized she'd been much shorter the last time she'd seen him. He must never have been a big man in fact- she'd just seen him through the eyes of a child.

"Can I at least use the bathroom and get a glass of water?" He shifted on his feet, shifting the pack from one shoulder to another, then setting it down. Though she didn't feel sorry for him- how could she- she still couldn't quite turn him away.

Opening the door, she stepped back and made room for him to enter, resigned. "Hi, Dad."

"Hi, Meredith." He stared at her, cleared his throat again, tried to smile. "Well. I did call, you know."

She turned away. "Don't call me sweetheart. Bathroom is down the hall."

"Thanks."

He took the satchel with him, closing the door quietly. She sat on her couch, closing her eyes while she waited for a good twenty minutes. When was the last time they'd spoken? Months ago. Water ran, the usual sounds of morning grooming. When he emerged, freshly shaved and in a new t-shirt, he looked neater if not less haggard.

"I hitchhiked here," he said. "The rest stops in this state aren't great. They used to be nicer."

"That was twenty years ago." Were they really going to do the small talk thing?

"Yeah. Do you mind if I sit down?"

"What do you want, Dad?"

Sighing, he crouched down in front of her. "I know you're mad at me, Mere-"

"Are you insane? Mad?" She shook her head. "I'm not mad. I just don't really want you here."

"You've become a beautiful woman, Meredith. Prettier than your mother."

Tears pricked her eyes, an echo of his sudden rapid blinking. She surged to her feet, hurrying to her bedroom. He didn't follow- if he had she probably would have kicked him out of her place then and there. Meredith took her time dressing and cleaning up. She felt better after the ritual soothed frazzled nerves. When she emerged from the bathroom, Harvey was sitting cross legged where she'd left him. He glanced up at her.

"Katherine called me when you graduated," he said. His eyes lowered, following the slump of his shoulders. "A teacher, huh? I missed all of that."

"I hope you don't want me to feel sorry for you."

His lips thinned, an expression she frequently saw in her own mirror. "No, I don't. What I did was inexcusable. I regret it every day of my life."

"You *shot* a man."

"It was an accident." He held up a hand. "An accident I caused. But I didn't go there intending on hurting that man. Roughing him up a little- but not hurting him."

"Killing him, you mean. Leaving his family without a husband and father." Her voice cracked. Leaving Liam without a father.

"I can't take that back. But I've paid my price. I lost my family, the best years of my life."

She shook her head. "I can't deal with this right now." A blanket of calm layered settled over confusion and the grim echoes of her childhood, of her automatic... wariness of him. Of his stress induced temper and dislike of anything *Bear.* Meredith glanced around for her purse, grabbing it off the hook where she'd hung it last night. "I'm going out. When I get back we can talk and figure out what you're going to do." After all, that's what she did. Help people straighten up their lives.

Harvey said nothing. She left the apartment, starting up her car and driving aimlessly, roads she'd traveled her whole life. Traffic this time of day was low- most people were at church. Guilt pinged her- just a little. She probably needed to go to church. Lord knew she had sins to make up for, first of all being the catalyst of her father's horrible actions that day.

Because if it hadn't been for her, he never would have confronted Conroy that day.

The only place she ever went when she needed peace was the garden. The earth calmed her nerves, familiar tasks requiring just enough attention that she could think peacefully, or let her thoughts go and be silent.

"Hey, teach."

Meredith glanced up and smiled. Well, she wasn't the only one who retreated to the gardens when her thoughts were troubled.

"Shouldn't you be in Sunday school?" she asked Brick, arching an eyebrow. The teenager snorted, knowing she was teasing.

"I'll go when you go." Brick sat on a nearby bench. Meredith noticed a wide book in the girl's hands.

"What's that?"

"Library book. I wanted to read up on winter gardens. I thought we could try to build greenhouses this year. They aren't expensive. Some pipe and plastic."

Meredith nodded. "You read my mind. I had plans to talk to you guys about it this week. If we decide to grow winter greens, we need to start our seeds."

Brick read, leafing through pages and making occasional comments while Meredith worked. The sun continued to rise, heating up the air past pleasant warm and back into uncomfortable hot.

"I need something to drink," Meredith said, swiping a hand across her forehead. Sweaty. Ugh.

"My timing is perfect, then."

She would have jumped, but Brick's quick glance over Meredith's shoulder provided a few seconds warning. She rose, wiping hands on her thighs, and turned.

Liam held two tumblers of what looked like homemade lemonade. It wasn't a commercial bright yellow, and real slices of lemon floated in the bottom.

"Bless you," she said, forgetting her nervousness, forgetting her reservations, and nearly lunging for the glass. He handed the second tumbler to Brick, who nodded her thanks. "Oh, this is good. Ginger and cayenne?"

He smiled. "Good buds. I have to kick it up a notch."

Meredith laughed. "This isn't Grandma's lemonade, that's for sure. What brings you out on a Sunday?"

Her smile faded as she remembered the reason she was out on a Sunday.

"Hey," he said, watching her. "What's wrong? You were just smiling."

She looked at the pile of tools at her feet, shaking her head. "Nothing. Just my own issues."

Liam slung an arm around her shoulders, turning her towards the bench. Brick scooted over, eyes narrowed.

"You want to talk about it?" he asked.

"No."

"Then talk to me about the class. As a matter of fact why don't we go back to my place and have lunch. You, too," he said to Brick. "I could use a student's perspective as well."

Meredith hesitated. If he'd just invited her, her answer would have been a flat out refusal. But Brick was watching, and Meredith was conscious of the importance for the girl to participate in as many positive social interactions with adults as possible.

"Okay. Let me go in my office and grab my planner and notebooks."

"So..." Liam turned to the human teenager. "Have you been with Teens and Greens long?"

The girl shrugged, eyeing him sideways. "About two years."

"Do you like it?"

She turned her head to face him fully, lip curling. "I'm still here, aren't I?"

Spare him from the scorn of children. "Seems like it. Is Meredith a good teacher?" The girl- Brick? That couldn't be her name- frowned at him.

"Why don't you let the garden tell you whether she's a good teacher. We make money with our produce. And it tastes good, too."

"Huh." He supposed that logic made sense. As a chef, the proof of his skill was on the plate. Standing, he wandered further into the garden, taking a closer look at various plants.

"So are you going to kick us out?" the girl asked. He turned around, studying her. She was on her feet now, arms folded nonchalantly. But her eyes were a little too serious, belying the casual pose.

"It means a lot to you, doesn't it? Most teenagers would be somewhere fun on a weekend."

"You're a frou frou chef and growing real food isn't fun to you?"

Liam laughed. "It is to *me*. But I'm a bit older than you." He studied her, considering. "Or is it that there just isn't anywhere fun in this small place to go?"

She shrugged, looking down. Liam dropped the subject, sensing something was wrong- but it wasn't his business.

"So you kicking us out or what? You changed the subject."

"No, I'm not kicking you out. Meredith and I are going to work out an arrangement."

"Cool." Her head rose. "Do you like her?"

"What?"

She tilted her head, hacked off dark hair brushing thin shoulders. "I'm not stupid. And I'm not a kid. But she doesn't date much, so maybe you wanna leave her alone."

Really. "I think I'd like to get to know her better. She seems... interesting."

"Yeah. Well, just make sure when you're getting to *know* her better, you're treating her decent. She doesn't deserve to be played."

Was this how normal teenage girls talked? He couldn't remember ever having this kind of conversation with a kid before.

"I don't play games, and I don't want to hurt her."

"Cool. Why don't I give you a tour?"

They spent the next several minutes going through the various plants in the garden. Brick was knowledgeable, talking with a confidence that demanded respect. Both for her, and for her teacher.

After a while Liam looked back towards the building. "I'm going to go see what's taking Meredith so long," he said. "She may have decided to skip out on us." He didn't really know her, but his Bear already had a good feel for the woman's personality. And as a man, he recognized her reluctant attraction for what it was. She leaned to close to the skittish side of the female spectrum for his comfort. He couldn't court a woman who didn't want to be courted. Well, he *could*. It would just make things more difficult.

She'd escaped into her office, walking fast. Considered texting Brick a quick message to abandon ship while Liam was unaware. Her thumbs hovered over the cell before she slid it back into her pocket with a sigh. It would probably be worse to have to explain to her future boss why she had snuck away. Better to just ride out this attraction until its end. He might imply his Bear was prodding him towards her, but Meredith wasn't quite sure she believed it. He'd seen her for the first time, what, three days ago? Meredith didn't believe in instalove, or even instalust. Though her previously dormant body was doing its best to convince her otherwise.

Instead she texted Tamar, asking if she thought it was a good idea to go to Liam's house. Her friend pinged her back almost immediately.

:Be careful. The Alpha's are even more controlling than the rank and file. I'll text you when I get off.:

Picking up her notebooks and planner, she left the office, running into Sheane on the way out. The Director was dressed in leggings and a loose t-shirt, hair pulled back.

"Workout?" Meredith asked. Sunday was the quietest day to use the equipment in the basement.

Sheane smiled. "More out than work, but I made myself do sixty minutes on the bike."

"Gardening is my cardio."

"And speaking of, have you spoken with Mr. Conroy yet?"

Meredith realized she hadn't updated Sheane on any of the events of the previous few days. She chalked it up to the distraction of dealing with her father and Liam at the same time. They began walking towards the doors.

"Yes, and he's going to let us stay, with some conditions."

"That's excellent news. What are the conditions?"

"He wants me to absorb his students and co-teach a class. I guess good chefs grow their own produce."

"Clever." Sheane glanced at her, frowning. "Meredith, does he know who your father is?"

Meredith stopped, mouth firming. "No. And I'm not going to tell him. Neither are you."

"Is that smart? This is a small town."

"I know- but even if he figures it out, by that time he'll know I'm not my father." Meredith chewed on her bottom lip. "Besides, I'm *tired* of that one horrible day hanging over me."

Sheane's eyes were steady. "You still haven't dealt with it. All your friends have left this town- but you've stayed behind. There's a reason for that."

"I- the kids-"

"Are an excuse. I think you should tell him. You will never be able to move on until you confront your issues."

Meredith closed her eyes. "I still feel guilty. I was such a spoiled brat. If I hadn't been so demanding, my father wouldn't have snapped when he lost the farm to Liam's dad."

"That's bullshit. All little girls are demanding. They want fancy clothes, makeup, dance lessons." She took Meredith's hand, squeezing. "It's the parent's job to either provide it or teach the children to do without. You didn't make your father confront Kyle Conroy."

"But-"

The Director glared. "You didn't make your father bring a loaded shotgun to the confrontation. You didn't make him start a physical altercation and cause the trigger to go off."

Intellectually Meredith knew Sheane was right. If one of her teenagers had come to her with similar issues, Meredith's temper would have burst. A child wasn't to blame for the actions of an adult. But that didn't stop her from feeling emotionally responsible. It didn't stop her from feeling shame.

"Tell him, Meredith," Sheane said, releasing her. "He isn't a bitter, stupid man. He might be upset at first- that's normal- but no one in their right mind would hold something like that against you."

"I'll think about it."

"Tell me what?" Liam asked when the red head Meredith turned the corner.

He'd caught the tail end of the conversation, more curious than suspicious. He couldn't imagine this lush little human had many deep, dark secrets to divulge.

The curvy beauty stopped short, verdant green eyes widening. He leaned against a wall, affecting a stern expression, crossing his arms. Poor woman looked... spooked. He felt a little bad for scaring her- but not that bad. The vivid expressions crossing her face were adorable. A word he never thought he'd use to describe *any* female, much less a human one.

"Uh- uh, well, see-" she stammered. It amused him, how terrible a liar she was. He supposed he should work up the concern to care what it was the director thought Meredith should tell him- but it didn't matter.

"Meredith?" He took a step forward. She backed away, an instinctive reaction that *did* bother him. A little feminine discomfort... excited him. True fear was nothing better than an insult. He would never hurt her.

Liam shifted, bracketing her against the wall in the cage of his arms. "Don't back away from me," he growled, then deliberately pitched his tone to a low croon. "I'll only hurt you if you ask me. Nicely."

Her heart lurched. He heard the rapid beat, saw the pulse in her graceful neck and wanted to sink his teeth into the hollow, brand her, mark her. The desire shook him, the strength of the Bear's demand that he make her his. Permanently. Liam's cock, always at half-mast around her, swelled, rubbing painfully against the fabric of his jeans.

He gritted his teeth and indulged himself, lowering his head into her hair and inhaling the earthy floral scent of nervous, nubile woman. Young, lush, vibrant woman. Enough innocence to allow for blushing, enough experience to heat her eyes to knowing pools of dark jade. His woman, damnit.

"Well, Meredith? What is it you needed to tell me?"

Feminine fingers pushed at his chest. He wanted to laugh. Did she think she could move him if he didn't want to be moved?

"Only that I intend to fight to keep you from kicking us out," she growled.

Hmm. "Well, if you plan to do that you should get in good with the owner."

She stopped pushing at him. "What?"

Liam's head rose. He shifted his hips, ensuring he didn't frighten her with his want. His mouth brushed the line of her jaw.

"What are you doing?" she squeaked.

"Helping you get in good with the owner."

He took her lips in a kiss, tasting the brown sugar gloss on her skin. Her mouth opened beneath his, body softening. Triumph surged, satisfaction. She wanted him though she probably told herself she didn't. But her soft flesh didn't lie. The barest arch of her back as she pressed against him didn't lie. She shuddered, and tried to hide the telltale movement.

Liam couldn't help himself; his hands slid around her waist to her buttocks, palming the plush globes and pulling her tight against him. He wanted to tear away her pants, wrap her legs around his waist and plunge into that little pussy, fuck her senseless right there against the wall of *his* building. Hear her scream his name as she bounced on his hips, fire hair covering them both.

He tore his mouth away, backing off. He had to get a grip of himself. The Bear roared in fury, protest. It wanted the woman. The woman belonged to them. Take the woman. Take the-

Liam whirled away. "I'll wait for you outside.

"You're not supposed to be texting at work."

Tamar jumped, shrieking. Her fingers scrambled not the drop the cell phone. Lord knew she couldn't afford to replace it.

Whirling around, she glared at Alphonso standing behind her, muscled arms crossed. She wished he'd put on a shirt with sleeves. Damn showoff.

"Stop sneaking up on me, Al," she demanded. "That shit is creepy." The Bear didn't make a damn sound, and he wore biker boots. In the middle of summer.

"I wasn't sneaking. You were busy texting."

She shoved the cell into her snug denim pocket, longing a brief moment for her comfy sweats at home. Couldn't wear those here. Maximizing tip potential meant giving the men who came in here- Bear and human- something to watch when she passed by. And with baby enhanced breasts, hips and ass like hers, there was plenty to watch.

Tamar glared. Why did he always stand so close? "Most people get breaks, you know."

"The same people who are unemployed?"

She pushed past him, trying to bump him into the wall. Bastard didn't budge. "You're such a jerk."

He muttered something under his breath. She stopped. "What?"

"You heard me. Get back on the damn floor." Alphonso brushed by her, not bothering to avoid rubbing up against her body.

"It's not even busy on Sunday," she yelled after him. It's why she'd been able to take a break. Fucking sexual harassment, side touching her like that. Except that when his arm and hip brushed hers, her body shivered. Damn, if she'd been her old self, she would have given that man a ride of his life.

She'd always been selective, but the ones she selected never regretted it.

Especially the ones who said things such as, "You know you like it" under their breath

CHAPTER

6

Meredith saw evidence of love in the freshly restored porch and attempt at landscaping. The house needed painting, though, and only about half the windows were new. She wondered at the gradual restoration because she knew for a fact the man wasn't cash poor.

"Do you like it?" Liam asked, reading her expression as she took in the newly planted shrubs and wildflowers lining the walkway. "It's my off day project."

She looked around, shading her eyes with her hand, avoiding his face. Her entire body felt... shaky. When she'd emerged from the building after an escape to the ladies room, he'd been waiting for her in the parking lot as if nothing had even happened. Ignoring that he'd almost ravished her in the middle of the hall.

"You've been doing this all by yourself?" Brick asked.

He led them around back. "Yeah. I like to work with my hands. It's satisfying to see it come to life bit by bit- hiring a contractor seems like cheating."

It made an odd kind of sense. He was a man who constructed flavors for a living; both a science and an art. He would need the control that came along with handling the work by himself.

Liam opened the tall wooden gate and gestured for them to precede him. Meredith stepped inside the yard. He did, indeed, have a basic kitchen garden. A few rows of carrots, a tall tomato plant, and several varieties of herbs. A lawn set was laid out in front of a fireplace.

The kitchen was about what she expected from a professional chef. Granite counter tops and some kind of rough stone she couldn't identify on the floor. White cabinets and appliances that looked as if they were designed by NASA.

"Do you have a taste for anything?" he asked, peering into his fridge. "Take a seat, be comfortable."

"I could go for grilled cheese," Brick said as the girls sat down on stools surrounding an island.

"I can make a grilled cheese unlike any you've ever had," he promised.

"With mushrooms."

"A woman after my own heart."

"Oh yeah?" Brick leaned her elbow on the counter. "Maybe we can get wild and crazy and add, I dunno, grilled onions."

Liam grinned. "Wild and crazy it is. What about you?"

Meredith met his eyes, finally. The warmth in them caressed her. For a moment she allowed herself to pretend they were just a small family relaxing on a Sunday afternoon, having lunch.

"I'll have whatever you want me to have," she replied, softly. His brow rose.

"Well, in that case..."

Meredith blushed, cursing herself. Remembering the dark promise on his face when he'd kissed her. Brick's face screwed up. "Gross. I'll pretend I didn't hear the blatant innuendo in that."

"I have no idea what you're talking about," Liam said, pulling out a cutting board, knife and several vegetables. And a hunk of cheese that didn't look like it came from the average Super Saver. "There's a pitcher of tea in the fridge."

He sliced a pepper lengthwise. Meredith didn't move, watching the skill he displayed with fascination. Turned on by the grace and power of his hands. If he could handle a fruit like that...

"Earth to Meredith," Brick said in her ear.

"What?"

She shook her head, sliding off her stool to go to the fridge. Meredith managed to not blush, mostly because she avoided all eyes. Her thighs pressed together, blood between her legs causing her flesh to throb. Liam's chopping increased in speed.

The sandwiches he grilled were delicious, especially when paired with an orange sorbet he pulled from the freezer.

"You mind if I go outside?" Brick asked Liam when they finished eating.

"No, make yourself at home."

Silence descended once the teen left. Meredith cleared her throat. "You cooked. I should clean up."

He leaned against the counter, folding his arms. "I didn't make much of a mess."

"No."

They stared at each other. "Come here," he said, voice lowering. A command, not a request, his eyes heated pools of ore.

Meredith slid off the stool, caught in his gaze, walking around the island to stand in front of him. He reached out, sliding hands around her waist and pulling her against him.

"You've had time to think," he said, and kissed her.

Her hands buried in his hair, gripping the strands with a sudden wild desperation. They tried to slide through her fingers, rough silk. Again his kiss dominate her senses, a wildness inside him she couldn't hope to handle- only hang on for the ride.

"There are so many reasons why this isn't a good idea," Meredith said, tearing her mouth away.

Liam's hand slid around the back of her neck, pinning her as a growl slipped from between his teeth.

"Too late. My house, my food- my woman."

Her core melted, a shiver of need throughout her body. Her breasts tightened, nipples hardening in reaction or anticipation, she couldn't tell. Liam lowered his head, tongue plunging into her mouth in a rhythm that echoed the intent of the hard length pulsing against her middle. She wanted to wrap her legs around his waist and just... rub all over him, a growing desperation that sent all rational thought fleeing.

His mouth trailed down the side of her throat, strong teeth nipping her delicate skin, not quite gentle.

"Liam," she gasped, arching against him as breath tickled the inside of her ear. "Oh!"

"We have to stop," he said, arm tightening around her waist in a conflicting message. "Or I'm going to fuck you right here."

Which- wouldn't be a good idea. Right? He was as hard as a rock, as hard as a-

"Shit." Meredith rarely cursed, but the word translated from thought to speech. She made herself pull away, mostly because Liam was already letting her go. "Brick."

He smirked. "That's a smart kid. I'm pretty sure she's still outside."

"Liam- what are we doing?"

"What do you want to be doing?" His eyes shut for a moment, a shudder racking the tall, strong body. When he opened them, some of the heat banked, ruthlessly pushed aside though she could tell his cock wasn't cooperating.

Meredith inhaled, steadying her nerves and resolve. "I- there's something you should know." She stepped out of his arms. Several feet, returning to her stool, but not sitting down. After a moment, he might not want her in his house at all.

Liam watched her. "What's wrong, sweetheart? I told you you could talk about it if you wanted."

"There's something you should know about my... family."

He leaned back, folding his arms. "Are you all convicts?"

When she failed to respond, his brow rose. "Oookaay. Well, I know you're a licensed teacher, so I'm pretty sure *you* don't have a criminal record. Meredith, you aren't your family."

She stared at him, stony. "Do you really believe that? Don't we teach our students that you're defined by who your friends are?"

Liam frowned. "You can pick your friends. You can't pick your relatives."

"That's an excuse."

His gaze was steady. "Is that what you would tell Brick? That she can't rise above the poor choices of her relatives?"

Meredith opened her mouth, closed it. Looked down at her feet. She didn't hear him move, but a long finger tapped her chin, raising her head to meet his eyes.

"I know *you*, Meredith. A woman who works hard, cares about other people and tries to make a difference. A woman who places her fears aside for the greater good."

She blinked rapidly. "You make me sound like a good person. I'm not. I'm spoiled and selfish-"

Liam laughed.

"Is something funny?" she demanded, rubbing her eye furiously. She must have gotten a lash stuck in it.

"You are. I haven't seen a speck of selfishness in you yet." He grinned down at her. "But then, we have yet to fight over the last slice of chocolate cake."

Meredith sniffed. "Chocolate cake is overdone. It will take something far more exotic to impress me."

He lowered his face to hers. "Is that a challenge?"

She shrugged with one shoulder. "You can take it however you want. But I still need to tell you-"

He placed a finger over her lips. Firmly. "I don't want to hear it," he said.

Her jaw firmed as she glared. "But-"

His expression hardened, a picture of obstinacy. "I don't want to hear it, Meredith. Unless you're about to confess you have a stable of nubile youths waiting to do your every naked deed..."

She gasped. "Liam!"

Oh, the cruelty in the knowing, sensual curve of his lips. "Well then, whatever you think you need to tell me isn't as bad as that, so I don't want to hear it. If it really is a problem, I'm sure I'll find out the hard way."

Meredith bit her lip, frustrated. "You like the hard way?" she snapped, irritated by his, just, *blasé* attitude.

"I love the hard way." He stepped towards her, lumbering grace. "I insist on the hard way. I will show you the hard way-"

"Oh my God, teenager incoming," Brick said loudly, stomping

through the back door. "Protect my innocent ears. I beg you."

Meredith sighed, turning around. "Your timing is perfect anyway. I was just about to give him a piece of my mind."

Brick snorted. "Sure you were."

As much as Meredith wanted to stay, she couldn't. Liam seemed willing to have them hang out at his place all day, but she insisted on getting Brick home.

"I know you have homework that you put off to the last minute," she said firmly, directing the girl to the door. And she still had her father to deal with. She couldn't decide if she should press her confession with Liam, or let it ride. At least she could always say she'd tried, if he ever accused her of withholding.

They turned the corner of the house, bickering good-naturedly. Liam noticed the disturbance first. Meredith pulled up short at his sudden, vicious cursing.

"Liam!" Her head whipped towards him as he strode past her. Her eyes followed him and she gasped, hurrying forward.

All four of his tires sat on the rims, slashed.

"Who would do something like this?" Meredith exclaimed, crouching down. He inhaled, drawing air deep into his lungs. Grabbed her arm and pulled her away as he scanned the street.

"I don't know," he growled after a moment. "But when I scent him, I will find out."

He glanced at Meredith, attention moving briefly to Brick. Paused, turned to face the teenager fully, eyes suddenly keen.

"Brick?" He said her name softly.

Meredith turned, taking in the teenager's white, set expression and grim eyes.

"Brick, do you know something about this?"

The girl's expression said everything. Meredith rushed towards her and enveloped the stiff teenager in a hug. For a moment, a familiar dread lurked behind young-old eyes. A dread Meredith was all too familiar with.

"It's okay, whatever it is."

"Honey, is there something going on you want to tell me about?" Liam asked. Meredith partially released her student, turning so her arm was still slung around Brick's slender shoulders. Liam looked down at them both, incredulous anger gone.

Brick looked down. "The family I live with. They have a son around my age."

"Yes?"

"We... don't get along. He does little things to try and get me in trouble. He said he was going to do something big."

"Why?" Liam asked, still. Not even a strand of hair moved.

"He- before I lived in his house. We kinda knew each other from school. He's one of the more popular kids. Not too much, just average. But more popular than me, you know? He said he liked me a little."

A ball of sickness unfurled in Meredith's stomach. And anger, welling up from somewhere deep and ugly. "Has he tried to hurt you, Brick?"

The girl said nothing.

"I'll *kill* him." Fury bubbled over. "Is he the one you were in a 'fight' with? Did he hit you?"

"It was self-defense," Brick snapped. "And I almost broke his pussy ass arm. That's why he's been doing bullshit stuff. He probably figured you'd blame me for this cause of my vandalism record." She paused. "He's a little stupid."

"That means he followed you, Brick," Liam said. Meredith glanced back up at Liam, froze. A small, relaxed smile played around his mouth. His eyes looked... happy, crinkled at the edges. White teeth gleaming. "Tell you what, why don't you tell me where he likes to hang out, and I'll go have a little chat, hmm? Nice and friendly."

Meredith licked her lips. "I'm coming with you." No, no. That was the wrong thing to say. She'd meant to tell Liam to not do anything foolish. To be calm and mature. The smiling expression didn't fool her for one second. But instead, a part of her reveled at the violence lurking beneath the facade. Approved and wanted to participate.

Liam looked at her, knowing. Approving. "I think you should stay with Brick this time, for moral support."

Brick muttered something under her breath. Liam's brow shot up.

"What? What did she say?" Meredith asked.

"Plausible deniability."

Brick told him the park her foster brother liked to hang out at. He looked for the kid, a tall, lanky teen with longish blond hair and glasses, skateboard propped at his side. His friends saw him coming first, scattering when Liam bared his teeth. The boy's eyes widened. Liam bounded forward, grabbing him before he, too, could disappear like a roach.

Liam grabbed the boy's wrist and shoulder, twisting it up to his back, thrusting him against the wall of the park building. The thud of the boy's cheek hitting cement echoed his startled cry.

"What the fuck, man? Get the fuck off me, you fucking bastard. Who the fuck the hell are you?"

Such erudite language. The teenager squirmed, Liam's elbow against this back as he picked the boy off his toes, wrenching his shoulder.

"Don't act like you don't recognize me, you little shit." The teenager's squeals quieted. "I'm a friend of Brick's and the punk ass stunt you pulled didn't do shit but piss me off. If I find out you've bothered her again, this…" Liam wrenched upward, eliciting a high pitched howl "…will be the least of the pain I inflict on you. And it won't be the man you will face, but the Bear. Nod if you understand."

The boy nodded, frantic.

"Good. Glad we had this discussion."

CHAPTER

7

Liam needed a drink after
dealing with the boy. The one place he
felt comfortable enough to relax was
Alphonso's. His second worked the bar
on the occasional whim, retreating from
the door post, claiming it was relaxing.
Whatever. If Liam wasn't working on his
house, his idea of relaxation was more

along the lines of menu planning. But that was him. And, of course, now there was Meredith.

He took a sip of the dark, foamy beer, anticipation tensing his muscles. He forced himself to relax. Sip.

"In that deep already, huh?"

Alphonso wiped a clean rag along the counter near Liam, then set it aside. Someone picked a rock classic from the fancy digital jukebox.

"We're still getting to know each other."

"Right." Long eyes narrowed. "You only drink when you're dealing with a woman."

"The restaurant is my woman."

"Not anymore. Your mother happy?"

He hadn't talked to her about it in any depth. "I'm doing what they asked me to do. Finding a human woman to mate."

"And then comes the babies in the baby carriage."

It hit him hard, an image of Meredith rounded with his cub. Another of her holding a swaddled infant in her arms, sitting in a comfortable chair in their garden. He smiled. Where had all those plants come from? The woman was taking over his growing space even in his imagination.

"Shit. You've got it bad, man."

Liam looked up, not denying it. Alphonso watched him carefully. "What does your Bear say?"

"You already know the Bear is driving this." Except... he liked Meredith. As a man, as himself. A little timid, but brave when it counted. Passion under her reserved surface.

"What's her name again?"

"Meredith." Liam frowned, realizing he didn't know her last name. "I don't know her last name."

"Yeah, I just wanted to know if you knew. I'll find out for you. Look bad if you ask her. She'll think you weren't paying attention."

Liam grimaced. They hadn't gotten around to last names, though he knew all the information was in her lease file. She knew his, though. She'd called him Mr. Conroy plenty of times. Huh. Maybe he should let Alphonso find out the little things, so Liam could play it off like he'd been doing his homework all along. Weren't women flattered when they thought you were checking them out?

"Okay. See what you can dig up. Her favorite color and all that stuff."

"Have you even had a conversation with her that wasn't about food or plants?"

"Of course." He just couldn't remember about what. He'd have to change that, though. There would have to be conversations. And then, after the conversations...

"Has she seen you shift?" Alphonso shook his head when Liam didn't respond. "You can't put that off, man. Better to know right now if she can handle it, or if she's the freak out type."

A woman willing to defend her cub- and the girl Brick was Meredith's cub- with violence wouldn't be scared of a Bear. But he knew Alphonso was right. Liam would have to make plans to take her somewhere quiet and private and show her his other side.

Meredith reluctantly allowed Liam to take care of the issue. Not just because he was a tall, scary looking man when he wanted to be, but because she needed to keep her hands somewhat clean to run Teens and Greens. She could just imagine what would happen to what little state funding she received if she went to jail for beating up a teenager, no matter how well deserved.

Still, she pulled Brick aside after two days of what she considered to be flawless patience.

"Is everything okay at home? Did Liam help at all?" Meredith asked her.

The teen looked uncomfortable. "Uh... Liam and I kinda decided to keep it on the down lo, you know."

Meredith gaped. "Do you mean you two handled this together and are keeping me out of the loop?"

Brick stared at her. "Yeah, that's what I said. It was, like, English and everything."

Meredith blew out a breath and tried to be stern. "Don't sass. It's a bad habit."

"Meredith."

She turned at the familiar male voice. Moody golden eyes stared at her. "Hi, Al. Brick, why don't you go on out to the garden? I'll follow in a minute."

She didn't hear footsteps, and looked over her shoulder. The teenager stood, eyes narrowed. "Brick?"

After a moment Brick shrugged and made her way out of the building.

"What's up?" Meredith asked her best friend's boss. Tall, lean muscled shoulders shown off by a sleeveless t-shirt. Scruffy, fitted jeans and glossy dark hair. She patted her red braid, wishing she could brush it into that kind of sleek obedience.

"Liam asked me to walk through the building and ask a few questions."

It was the first time she'd seen Al outside of the shadows of his bar except for the other day. He must be friends with Liam- they were both werebears, so it made sense. "Sure. I can give you a tour. We'll start in the kitchens, since that seems to be the most important place."

"Thank you."

She led him through the halls at a brisk pace. "When will the crews start work? I believe Mr. Conroy had some plans to begin the renovations soon."

"Soon. He's just finalizing design plans now. The crews will begin demo shortly. You know, Tamar never mentioned your last name."

She slanted him a glance. Why would she? "Tyler. You know I run an afterschool enrichment program here? Here are the kitchens."

He asked a few questions, made notations in his cell. Meredith remembered the days of pads and paper. Now everyone took notes on their devices.

"How long have you run Teens and Greens?" he asked with the voice of a man making polite small talk. She wanted to tell him not to bother- she'd seen his idea of small talk when tossing drunks out of his bar- or barking orders at Tamar. But Meredith obliged him, discussing the program. She showed him the conference and workout rooms in the basement, directed him to the restrooms which were clean but old.

"What colors would you like in the bathrooms?"

Meredith blinked. Alphonso smirked. "Liam asked me to get a girl's input before the finishes were chosen. The designer is male, too."

"That's smart. Well, neutrals are always nice for a spa like feel. Warm browns with natural stone finishes. Maybe some dark wood accents."

"Sounds sophisticated."

They made their way around to the front entrance. "Well, that's all there is, Alphonso. If there aren't any other questions, I should really get out to my kids."

"No problem." He held out a hand. "If you think of anything else, just come by the bar."

She took his hand, shaking it, wondering at the oddness of his behavior. He was being downright... civilized. "Of course. You have my number if you-"

His hand convulsed over hers. Meredith jerked, startled, but he wasn't paying attention to her, looking over her shoulders, expression tight.

"Al," she said, snapped. He dropped her hand a split second later. Meredith turned around to see what had him so bothered and stilled.

"Dad!"

Harvey stood just inside the entrance, hands in his pockets, looking between her and Alphonso.

"I wanted to see where you worked, Mere."

She hurried towards him. "I thought we agreed you'd stay in the apartment and not wander around town." Until she figured out what to do with him.

"You know I can't do that, Mere. I have to check in with the parole officer, and I need to find a job. I can't sleep on your couch forever."

No, he couldn't. She remembered Alphonso's presence at her back. She turned on her heels, hairs on her neck rising, encountering a smooth expression. Smooth, and cool. He nodded at Meredith and walked past them without another word and out of the building.

"Who was that, Mere?"

She frowned. Something was bothering her, but she couldn't quite pinpoint what. "Don't worry about it, Dad. Do you have a bus card? You should get back home before anyone sees you."

Before anyone who knew Liam, and knew her, saw him. The fact that she was... dating the restaurateur still surprised her during times of quiet reflection. The last week had been a delightful dance of conversation, passion, and occasional companionable silences. They'd been able to explore each other's interest while Meredith managed to keep conversations away from the past. And managed to make excuses for why he couldn't come by her apartment. Mostly by claiming she was ashamed because it was small and not very pretty.

The expression around his eyes tightened. "I know you're ashamed of me."

She gritted her teeth, then felt ashamed of her response. Then felt ashamed for feeling ashamed.

"Dad, you weren't the most loving parent when I was growing up... before you shot a man. And yes, I am ashamed of that. But you know what? You have to deal with it. So do I. I just want you to start living your life so I can go back to mine."

She turned away, knowing it was harsh. But she hadn't asked for her entire childhood to be destroyed, and not just hers. And she was a little sick of her own inner whining about it. Meredith waited until she heard the door close and then banished him from her mind. She had a garden to run.

Alphonso considered himself a fair man. Shit happened to everyone, and usually the innocent paid the worst price. So when he realized the man talking to Meredith was Harvey Tyler, and he was apparently Meredith's father, he decided not to make any rash decisions. Like run off and tell Liam. Right away.

Liam didn't necessarily need to know.

He swiped a rag over the counter for show, glancing at Tamar. She met his eyes, hip cocked as she took a lunch order. They didn't get a ton of lunch business, their beer being several notches better than their... food. He supposed he should do something about that just to be professional, but they made enough money during the evenings and weekends he figured there was no reason to buck the system.

Tamar came to him a minute later. "You rang?"

That's why he liked the woman. She was the perfect employee— showed up in a low cut blouse, smiled, worked hard and didn't give the customers flack. And she seemed to read his mind. Interesting, with a human. They were usually as deaf as his socks when it came to reading body language. But he supposed having grown up together accounted for some, if not most, of the familiarity. Which made the fact she was the perfect employee- except for the constant lip- even more astonishing.

"You're friends with Meredith Tyler, right?"

Rich russet eyes slid away from his. "Yeeaahhh."

"You sound like you aren't sure."

He watched her run a tongue around her teeth. "I'm sure."

Interesting. So Tamar knew, and also knew better than to rat her friend out.

"Tell me about her. What's her angle?"

"Angle?" Tamar's full lips turned down. "Meredith is one of the kindest people I know. She didn't deserve that rat of a-"

"Don't stop on my account."

"I think my order is up," she said, voice flat. Alphonso watched her go- and watched her avoid his gaze- but let her go.

Man, Liam would be pissed when he realized he was the last one to know his woman was the daughter of the man who had murdered his father. Talk about some Romeo and Juliet fucked up shit. That's why he was never mating.

But his gaze rested on Tamar again, and he wasn't sure why it was always so hard to look away.

"It's good."

Meredith turned, straightening from her crouch where she'd been carefully packing the few remaining jars of salsa and preserves. Liam stood at the table, a sample spoon in his mouth.

"The teenagers make it every Friday evening," she said, keeping her voice even. She couldn't help how her heart spiked from the sight of him, how her core dampened, clamoring to take him behind one of the old brick buildings and... show him her vegetables.

His nostrils flared, eyes paling to a warm amber. "How many jars can they produce a week?"

She struggled to think. "We do twenty of each flavor. There's three flavors of salsa and three jams- one of them being a savory jam."

"I might be interested in carrying a line in the restaurant."

Her eyes widened, and she grinned. Brick bounded over, back from her trip with another student to the rented U-Haul.

"'Sup, Mr. Conroy," the girl greeted. She glanced at the jar in his hand. "Good, huh? You should serve it with chips in your restaurant on like a southwestern night or something. Instead of bread, you know?"

Liam looked at Brick thoughtfully. "I was discussing something similar with your teacher," he replied. "That isn't a bad idea." He looked at Meredith, lifting the jar. "I'll take whatever you have leftover."

She licked her lips. "No charge. Consider it samples. For a future order."

He titled his head, studying her with glowing were eyes. What was he feeling, thinking, that made his shifter nature so... evident... at the moment?

"Hmm. That wouldn't be fair. I'll take one of each flavor as a sample, and the rest I'll pay retail for."

"Take one of each as a sample," she countered, "and the rest at wholesale. You should pass out samples to your customers, see if they like it before you place an order."

She folded her arms.

He smiled at her, a slow, masculine expression filled with a heat that struck a chord deep in her body. Ringing bells.

"Tell you what. We'll do it your way- but there's a price."

She watched him warily. "A price."

"A kiss."

Meredith tensed. His kisses weren't nearly as benign as he made them sound. One kiss would leave her achy with need the rest of the damn day. And all night, until she was one thought away from texting him. And she'd never engaged in a late night booty call in her life. She blushed. Dark eyes watched her, knowing.

"Come here, Meredith."

"There's people around."

"I'll be quick."

Her feet took her to him before her mind could agree. Traitors. He didn't wait for permission, wrapping a strong hand around the back of her neck, soft lisp descending on hers in a deep, drugging kiss. Stealing her breath, her will to resist.

"I'll let you know what they think," he said, pulling away.

"I'll box them up for you," Brick said, making Meredith jump. She hadn't realized the girl was behind her.

"Oh! Yes- um. That would be... good."

Brick snorted, muttering under her breath. She jerked her head at one of the other students, a young man with a wide grin on his face. The color on Meredith's cheeks deepened. It was all she could do to make her feet move and help them; to break the forbidden spell of Liam Conroy and this strange attraction between them.

She hauled the second to last box into her arms, having shooed Liam away minutes ago. This was her work- she didn't need him being all He-Bear on her like she wasn't capable of moving her own stock. Though his old-fashioned insistence was nice, along with the disgruntled though gentlemanly deference to her wishes when he finally gave up and let her carry her own boxes.

The sound of glass shattering jerked her attention back to present time. She turned, glimpsing Brick's pale face before the girl burst into action, cleaning up the handful of jars she'd just dropped.

"No matter," Meredith said, crouching down to help with the glass. She glanced at the girl again, sunny smile fading. "Brick, it's just a few jars of preserves. It's okay."

The teenager shook her head. "I know. I'm cool."

Meredith sat back on her haunches. "You don't look cool. What's wrong?"

"Nothing."

But she saw the teenager's eyes flick over her shoulder, then jerk back down to the ground. She cut her finger picking up glass, letting out a string of curses.

"Brick," Meredith said, reproving.

"What, what? Jesus. It's just cuss words."

She opened her mouth to reply, but the girl cut her off, rising. "I said I'm fine!"

Meredith didn't think so.

CHAPTER
8

Meredith pressed Accept on her cell. Assigning Liam a ringtone she knew was a sign things were becoming serious. Still, most days shadowed her emotions as they dated, seeing each other nearly every evening and sometimes during the day, for the last two weeks.

"Hi."

"Sweetheart."

It warmed her when he called her that. Warmed her better than the sticky toffee pudding he'd made them for dessert the other night. She'd brought her five cheese and mushroom macaroni to his house. They'd taken to eating at least one meal together a day, even if it was just a quick sandwich at the Y. She saw him on site often, even heard him bellowing through the ruckus of the demo. She stayed outside as much as possible, and was relieved he wasn't touching her office to redecorate. At least not yet.

"Come camping with me tonight."

"Camping?" Not that she wasn't an outdoorsy kind of girl. But camping meant sleeping overnight, and that meant dark and privacy and a fluffy sleeping bag under a cozy tent... she licked her lips.

"Umm... who's doing the cooking?"

"Hebrew National, baby. Hebrew National."

It sounded delicious. "Okay."

"Do I need to bring two tents?" The soft promise in his voice shivered over her spine. Was she ready? When she was near him, it was all she could do to step back, to not tear off their clothes and fuck him senseless. But when she was in her right mind, she had to consider the consequences. To her heart. But damn, she was tired of being cautious.

"No. One is fine."

And as soon as she said the words, Meredith knew he would never let her take them back.

"Good." Warm, dark approval. "I'll pick you up?"

"No, I can meet you at the campsite."

"Meredith." The steel in his tone chased away the shivers. "I'll pick you up."

She closed her eyes, stifling a curse. Fine. She'd just have to make sure Harvey left soon.

"Dad, is there somewhere I can drop you off? How's the job hunt going?"

He looked up from the paper he was reading, uncomfortable with cruising Craigslist and the local want ads via internet.

"The program I'm in has a few leads for me."

She sat down at the table, forcing herself to be patient. It helped that the looming, angry, stressed man of her memories was absent in this average height, lean person with his soft voice and steady eyes.

"Is there somewhere you need to go?" she repeated, glancing at the DVR clock. Liam would be here soon, and it was getting harder and harder to keep him out of her apartment. She could tell from the raised eyebrow and slight frown he was trying to decide if she was keeping something from him.

She was, but not quite what any normal male would think she was keeping a secret.

"Thing is, Dad, I have a guest coming by to pick me up and, well..." Meredith felt a moment of discomfort. Her reluctance to hurt his feelings disturbed her sense of justice. Since when did the feelings of a killer matter?

"Who's this guest?" Harvey asked. "A friend?"

"Yes, a friend, and he'll be here soon-"

"He?" Harvey smiled, a rare occurrence, leaning an arm on the table. "Maybe I should meet him at the door then. Give him a look over."

She stared at him, half charitable mood evaporating. The image of the protective father with a shotgun ruined her mood.

"I don't think that's necessary." She paused, asking her mother to forgive her. "Have you talked to Mom yet? I told her you were staying with me- she didn't say anything but I think she'd like to see you." Kathy had never remarried. Never had much to say about Harvey at all.

He rose from the table, rolling up the newspaper. "Alright, sweetheart. I'll clear out so you don't have to explain your ex-convict Dad to your man."

Her lips thinned. He made it sound petty and inconsiderate.

"I'll introduce you if it gets serious, okay? I just don't think I should spring all my drama on him this early on."

"Makes sense." He hesitated, stooped slightly and kissed her on the forehead. "Enjoy yourself, Mere, and be careful."

He left out the door with his prepaid dollar store phone and a thin wallet, Meredith letting out a breath of relief. Then saw the clock and realized she was cutting it close.

Meredith walked out of her apartment as soon as he pulled up, a small backpack slung over her shoulder.

Walked fast. Liam's eyes narrowed. Not for the first time he wondered at her secret. He knew it wasn't simple vanity, like she'd claimed. Anger welled; he banished the emotion as ridiculous. There was no way she lived with another man; he refused to believe he was that bad a judge of character.

Her chili paste hair spilled in loose waves over her shoulders. As usual, green eyes looked at him through a half suspicious, half slumberous expression that kept him walking around with a perpetual hard on.

Not any longer. He'd given her time. Given her space to run away. She hadn't. He would make her his and ignore any more girly protests short of an actual 'no.' The faded jeans she wore hugged her hips, coyly demure with the deep v of her t-shirt, showing off more cleavage than he was comfortable letting his woman display. Her body was made for fucking, made for bearing his cubs. Made for him, the perfect armful of lush, sensual woman.

"Don't you have a sweater to put on?" he asked. The words just spilled out of his mouth without him editing for tone. He didn't want her to think he was unhappy with her appearance... he was just unhappy with so *much* of her appearance on display where other unmated males might bump into them.

She stopped in front of him, eyes narrowed. "What's wrong with what I have on?"

Shit. He knew that tone. "Nothing, sweetheart. I just don't want to have to kill a man for looking at what belongs to me."

Meredith stared at him. "That's ridiculous. That would never happen."

He bared his teeth at her. The creamy rose gold flesh swelled as she inhaled with irritation. Damn. He wanted to sink his face between the globes, tear off the shirt and bra and find out the color of her nipples. Fuck her plump ass from behind with his hands full of her breasts.

The little human took a step back, something flickering in her eyes. Not quite fear, but a feminine wariness. Yes. She should be wary. Very wary. He was no tame Alpha for her to play games with.

"I- I'll go grab a summer cardigan."

Wise.

Meredith watched Liam from the corner of her eyes. He wasn't in a bad mood, necessarily. But a tension rode him that hadn't been there when he'd pulled up. She'd seen him from her door, big body relaxed, a smile hovering on his lips. It was only when she came close that the smile disappeared, his hot dark eyes glued to her chest. If he was anyone else, she would have slapped him. The thoughts behind the stare... she shuddered, wondering if she would even get a hot dog tonight. Or if she was the menu.

She cleared her throat. "So... how was the restaurant today?" He'd mentioned earlier he'd be working a few hours though the schedule had him off. He'd mentioned, mouth quirked in wry humor, that his sister insisted he start leaving the staff in peace at least one day per week.

Liam glanced at her. "Small talk won't handle me, sweetheart. Only one thing will."

Well... that was clear enough. "Are we going to set up camp right away?"

He growled, and muttered something under his breath.

"What? Liam, did you just say-"

"That we might not make it to the camp site? You heard me." His teeth flashed. "Your hearing is getting much better. After tonight it will continue to improve."

What the hell did that mean? Did he think his cock was so magical it would give her new sense or something? Meredith blushed, feeling irritated she was such a Mary Sue that thinking the word 'cock' brought heat to her cheeks.

"A quarter for your thoughts," he purred. A Bear.

"It's a penny for your thoughts."

"Inflation, sweetheart."

They pulled into the campsite, a national park reserve right off the highway. Small campers and SUV's snuggled into slots. Children played on a small swingset near the edge of the lake. Meredith expected him to stop in one of the numbered slots, but he continued to drive up the narrow, winding dirt path.

"Where are we going?"

"The Den has land rights for private campgrounds a ways up. It's more private."

And, from the tone of his voice, they would need privacy. There was no actual slot to park in. He found a space of cleared land and sat the SUV there. Silence descended when the engine shut off. Meredith burst into motion, throwing off her seatbelt and hopping out of the car.

"What a nice day out. Is there a restroom near here or do we have to hike back down to the campgrounds? My, isn't it nice to have a bit of quiet."

She heard the driver door slam
and the subtle brush of fabric against...
what kind of metal were cars
constructed from anyway? Or were
they plastic? Not like the good old days,
huh, where everything was made in the
U.S.A. and-

"Meredith."

She jumped, shut her mouth,
realizing she was babbling, even her
thoughts were babbling. Could
thoughts babble? The heat of his body
pressed against her back as strong arms
wrapped around her. His body tensed
and for a split second she thought he
would push her onto her hands and
knees, pull down her pants and plunge
into her body. The hard length of him
against her back, his hands brushing the
undersides of her breasts, was proof
enough of his intentions.

But after a second, tension
eased.

"What are we going to do?" she asked, voice barely above a whisper.

Liam's breath caressed her ear as he kissed the lobe. "Whatever you want, sweetheart. I know you want. Need. I can smell your desire."

How mortifying. How arousing. She closed her eyes, hands rising to grip his wrists. Imagining those hands on her, the small of her back arched, an involuntary movement that sent the curve of her full bottom ever tighter against his cock. She couldn't help herself, some female instinct took over. Rubbing against him, pulling his hands to cup her breasts, wanting to feel the clever fingers pluck her nipples. Pluck her clit, sink into her pussy and fuck her until she came, and then wash rinse repeat with his cock.

Liam hissed, hands grasping flesh. He pulled away from her. "Wait, damnit, wait. Let me set up camp first."

Meredith allowed him to pull away, a slow smile on her lips. He sounded shaken, the words coming from between gritted teeth. She turned, watching as he avoided her eyes and headed to the trunk of the SUV.

He made short work of setting up the tent and sleeping bags. He also set out a small folding table and brought out supplies, including a portable grill. And more food than the two of them could possible eat on their own.

"Are we expecting company?" she asked him. "I thought it was just me and you."

His head turned towards her. Coal dark eyes speared her, though when he replied his voice was calm. "It's just you and me, but once we start cooking, others may smell and come investigate."

Meredith thought it was an interesting facet of their culture that he would pack food with the possibility of feeding unexpected guests in mind.

"Oh. Well. Maybe we shouldn't-do anything..." her voice trailed off as Liam rose, crossing the distance in a few graceful, lumbering steps. He swung her up into his arms, ignoring her small squeal of surprise. She was no tiny girl. He handled her as if she weighed nothing. Eyes devoured her as if she was the sexiest thing he'd ever seen.

His expression did that to her, released an inner sensuality kept under lock and key. Growing up, she'd endured her fair share of teasing. For being curvy, for being her father's daughter. Before she realized that the only standard of beauty that required women be skinny was the television standard. In real life, she'd never seen a man turn down a date with a full figured woman. And the skinny girls were *always* complaining about not being able to gain weight.

Besides, Liam was a big man. Alpha written over every line of his body. He'd crush a small girl. But a fiercely real woman like her- she could handle anything he could dish out.

Ducking into the tent, he lowered her to the ground with impressive control, pressing her into the soft sleeping bag, body covering hers. He held most of his weight on his forearms, but still the delicious weight of him, all hard body and not an ounce of flab, thrilled her. Meredith wrapped her legs around his waist, her hands around his neck, pulling his head down to hers.

"Kiss me," she demanded.

He laughed, teasing her by avoiding her seeking mouth. Teeth sank into the curve of her throat, edges sharper than she remembered. He pulled her back up onto her knees, the movement so fast she had to cling to his shoulders to keep her balance. Her shirt

ripped over her head, a rough urgency
fueling her lust.

She cupped her breasts in her
hands, pushing them up, watched with
dark eyes as the muscles under his face
shifted. As if the Bear was trying to peek
out. Devour her.

"Take the bra off," he said.
Meredith had no illusion it was a
request.

She reached behind her back,
fumbling with the hook as he watched,
hands on his thighs, coiled and ready to
pounce. She wondered if there was a
snake somewhere in his lineage. The
scrap of cotton fell to the ground, the
full globes of her flesh swinging free.
Liam inhaled. And moved, the grace
and strength of a Bear capturing its
prey.

His mouth found one nipple,
fingers plucking the other, tugging the
beaded flesh between his teeth.

Meredith moaned, a half gasp, half cry at the rough scrape of tongue and sharp edge of… fangs?

"Liam!" she squeaked, not quite panicking, but startled enough to pull away.

He snarled at her, lips drawing back to reveal lengthening incisors.

"Won't hurt you," he said. "Don't pull away."

She had to trust him. Without trust, there would be no relationship. How could he ever be himself with her if he knew she was frightened? She inhaled, forced her body to relax and leaned into him.

"I'm yours," she said. "Just don't mind me if I shriek a little."

He laughed, a deep broken chuff as he resumed the touches that sent fire into her clit and melted her core, juice waiting to coat his cock when he finally took her.

Her fingers fumbled, his desire for her enflaming her own, creating an uncharacteristic boldness. She tugged at buttons, impatient to undo the one by one. Liam let go of her for a moment, strong hands tearing the shirt from his body.

Rock hard flesh flexed under her fingers, satiny skin a temperature she thought might kill a human male. Her fingers roamed over the torso, feeling the strength and tension of his body, understanding she was about to allow that strength to unleash itself inside her. She would be helpless beneath him, no ability to make him stop if his strength was too much for her to Bear.

Her body didn't care about the danger. Her hand dipped underneath the band of his jeans, delving underneath silk to wrap around the thickness of his cock. It jumped in her fingers and Liam cried out.

"Fuck," he muttered. "Don't do that or I'll come. Want to come in your pussy. Or your mouth."

Licking her lips, "Why don't you then?"

His head snapped back, eyes flaring gold. "What? Don't play with me."

"Come in my mouth."

Liam stared at her, head tilted, muscles moving under his skin in a way that let her know she was dealing more with Bear, and less with man. He smiled, a slow revelation of fangs and dark, masculine satisfaction.

"Soon," he promised. "There are all kinds of things I'm going to do with you, and to you. But this first time will be for you."

"But I want-"

"Quiet." He put a finger over her mouth, then nudged her, tumbling her back onto the floor and tugging at her pants to peel them down her legs. "Fuck me. This is all mine."

CHAPTER

9

Air kissing her skin drove home the fact of her complete nakedness, legs splayed at his insistence, every inch of her flesh exposed in the early evening light to his regard. Every flaw of her complexion, the mother goddess feminine padding of her stomach and thighs. She saw no dimming of the heat.

In fact, he lowered himself down her body, eyes rolling up to watch her face, a faint stubble on his jaw rubbing against her skin.

"Mine to taste." His tongue played with her clit, hands draping her legs around his neck, voluntarily locking himself in. "Honey and heat and all fucking woman."

Meredith cried out. The texture of his tongue against her delicate flesh like millions of vibrating beads coaxing the blood to her clit, engorging with her desire. Liam took flesh between his teeth, tugging and licking, hands digging into the rounded globes of her ass to the point of delicious pain. He licked and tugged and rolled her in his mouth as pressure built and overflowed in a climax, tearing mewling cries of pleasure of her throat. His relentless drive to taste didn't stop there, tongue dipping even lower.

Shocked, she tried to rear back as his tongue, longer and wider and heavier than any human tongue had a right to be, speared her pussy, entering her in a rhythm that teased even more pleasure from her quivering body.

"Liam, please," she said in a broken voice. The pleasure was good, more than she'd ever had, but her body yearned for something... more. A possession that consumed and defiled and appeased that dark side of her nature begging to be fucked, hard and raw and dirty until she screamed loud enough the whole county knew her Bear was worshiping her.

"Please what, sweetheart?"

"Fuck me. I need your cock inside me." She swiped at him, feeling a beast rise up in her. He laughed, delighted.

He crawled back up her body. As soon as her hands touched his waistband she tugged clothing free of his body. His cock sprang out, the long, hard length a dark golden brown, veins pulsing with blood, the tip beaded with pre-cum. She licked her lips, eager and apprehensive, wondering if the advantage of having a Bear for a lover was also the disadvantage. Would her body accept something that huge inside her?

His pants gone, her hand wound his cock, positioning it at her entrance without her conscious thought. He looked at her, pressing the satiny head to her entrance, filling her. Her body stretched, a nearly painful pulling. She opened her legs wider, trying to open herself as he pressed in, inexorable, watching her with inhuman, implacable eyes.

She gasped, biting her lip, writhing beneath him. His cock rubbed a spot inside her as he sheathed himself to the hilt, giving her body barely a few seconds to adjust before he pulled out and entered her again, this time faster. And again and again until he was fucking her in a rhythm that bounced her tits and pushed her back into the ground.

Meredith's fingers clawed at his back, desperate for more, desperate for peace. "Liam," she cried as his hips shifted, finding a spot that sent a streak of lightning pleasure deep into her womb. "Oh, God."

"No, he corrected. "Liam. Alpha." He smiled. "Master, if you prefer."

She had the breath, the presence of mind, to half laugh, but it was close and soon she couldn't think at all. Her pussy stretching to fit him, slick with oil that aided his possession. He swelled in her even further and he switched from long, hard thrusts to a fast grind. Her body convulsed, climax sending her into temporary oblivion as her mind scrambled to process the pleasure.

He joined her a bare moment later, sheathed to the hilt, grinding against her cervix as hot jets of seed bathed her womb. He half collapsed on her and she reveled in his weight, his ragged breaths. She'd done this to him, her body bringing him to as great a climax as his had brought hers.

"Mine," he said, ragged.

Meredith flexed around him, wincing a little as he slowly pulled out.

"I don't know," she said, voice low and husky. "You might have to work to convince me."

His head jerked up, eyes widening as he looked in her face. Then he grinned, relaxing. "I'll spend all night convincing you, sweetheart. One of the advantages of having a Bear."

She thought about that for a moment, a little disturbed when the grin turned slightly evil as she paled, realizing the havoc that *all night* could wreak on her body. And her heart.

"I haven't seen your... Bear," she said.

He rolled over onto his back, bringing her with him, hands roaming over her bare skin and buttocks. He squeezed, cock hardening against her stomach.

"Already?"

Liam laughed. "All night long."

The muscles between her thighs ached come morning, mind blank from exhaustion. He let her sleep a few hours before waking her.

"Mere," he hissed in her ear, shaking her shoulder. "The sun is rising. Up, up!"

"Oh my God," she groaned, turning away from him. "I hate morning people."

"Deal with it. Come on, I have sweet stuff for breakfast."

That made her raise her head—lord knew she was a sucker for a breakfast pastry. "Oh yeah?"

Rolling onto her back, she pushed herself into a sitting position, pushing her long tangled hair behind her. He sat on his haunches in front of her, still, watching as she stretched.

Liam swore, started to set aside the paper bakery bag in his hand. She lunged, grabbing his wrist.

"You shall not pass unless I get my pastry," she swore. "No breakfast, no pussy."

"Wanna bet I can change your mind?" But he relented, giving her the bag with a sigh. She chewed on an apple cinnamon muffin.

"I need to wash up," she said, rising to her feet, unabashedly naked.

He rose with her. "There's a fast moving stream a quarter mile from here if you want to rough it."

That sounded... nice. Picturesque. She wrapped a towel around her body, stuffed her feet into her slip on walking shoes and carried her toiletry bag. They walked at a brisk pace- well, she walked at a brisk pace trying to keep up with Liam's strides. He slowed his pace after he noticed her trotting, slapping her on the ass with muttered, "shorty."

The stream was the width of two Liam's. She waded knee deep, folding the towel on a rock and carrying her soap into the water, spending a few minutes washing her sticky parts, enjoying the cold water bath.

Liam handed her a small bottle of water to brush her teeth, having anticipated her hesitance at rinsing her mouth with stream water. When she was clean and dry and her hair brushed out, he straightened from his slouch against a nearby tree.

"You said you wanted to see Bear," he said.

She stilled, looking at him, seeing the move of muscle under his face, the slow swelling of his shoulders as he undressed, eyes holding hers. Her heart kicked into high gear.

"Won't hurt you," he said, voice deepening. And then he... shifted, hands morphing into huge paws, back bending and twisting, haunches forming out of thighs as fur sprouted along his body. Faster and faster until the changes were so quick she couldn't follow them with her eyes.

His size took her breath away, a full ten feet when he rose tall on hind legs, chest wide and head thrown back. He fell forward onto four legs, the weight of him sending a small shockwave through the ground. She stumbled back a few steps, instinctively afraid. He stilled, head tilted, and waited.

Meredith controlled her fear, knowing that if she couldn't deal with this side of his nature, their relationship was doomed. Sunlight gleamed on glossy brown; black fur, dark eyes watching her with a calm intelligence no mere animal possessed.

She walked forward, forcing her feet to move one step at a time, remembering that this was the man whose body shed accepted into her own, multiple times and in multiple ways. The man who her heart was accepting. Her hands reached out, burying themselves in the fur around his neck.

"Oh my," she breathed. "This would come in real handy in the winter."

His nose bumped her shoulder.

"Ow."

He began to shift. She backed away, uncertain of her ability to not freak out if she stood that close during the process. It wasn't like it was every day she watched a man turn into a Bear and vice versa. Television always made it look so… romantic.

"Are you okay?" he asked when he stood before her, lean muscled body gleaming in the sunlight.

Meredith licked her lips. "Yeah, I'm okay. You're beautiful, you know. It will just take some getting used to."

He held out a hand. She went to him, taking the hand so he could draw her into the circle of his arms. His nose buried in her neck, chest expanding as he inhaled. She felt the growing jut of his erection against her middle and laughed, relaxing.

"You aren't a Bear, you're a rabbit."

"Let me convince you otherwise."

And he did.

She would have loved to spend the entire day with Liam, but she couldn't afford to cancel her classes. At twelve dollars per thirty minute class, the money added up pretty fast if she booked students back to back for four to five hours in a row. She texted her father a quick message while Liam drove her home, making sure Harvey wasn't in the apartment. When he replied that he was out, she exhaled a sigh of relief.

Liam glanced at her curiously. "Penny?"

"I was checking up on my schedule," she lied. "I wasn't sure what time my first class was today- but I'm good."

"Good." He pulled up into the parking lot, turned off the engine and hesitated. She frowned at him, at the odd sideways expression.

"What?"

His fingers tapped the steering wheel. "Meredith, you know if you need anything, any help, you can..." he trailed off, grimacing. "Spare me from independent women. Look, woman, if you think I'm going to let you-"

She held up a hand, struggling with a warring sense of pleasure and irritated pride. "I understand, and thank you for the offer. If I'm ever in a position where I'm about to lose the roof over my head or starve- which didn't happen even in college- I'll make an arrangement with you. Since you're rich and my rent is probably what you spend on kitchen gadgets every month."

He relaxed, grinned at her. "At least you know me well enough not to have said 'shoes.'"

She snorted. She didn't think he even owned a pair of closed toe shoes, except for the black restaurant shoes he wore at work.

He had her wait on him to open her door, wrapping an arm around her waist to lift her down the step, capturing her mouth in a kiss before reluctantly letting her go. His hand remained on the small of her back as they approached her front door. She fumbled through her purse for her keys.

"I need to get a smaller purse," she muttered. "It always takes so long-"

Liam's hand bunched in the shirt at her back, jerking her back an inch into his body. "Liam-"

"Who is he?" he snarled. She twisted, shocked by the violence in his tone. There was no warmth in his eyes, only diamond cold anger.

"W-what?" Meredith tried to pull away, but he held her, growling.

"I smell a man, he smells like you." He swore, igniting a tingle of fear. "Stop struggling." He lifted her off her feet, bringing her face to face with him.

"It's probably my father!" she cried out, having dropped the purse to clutch at his shoulders. "*Liam*."

The Alpha Bear put her down, gently, anger fading as he inhaled. "Your father? Father." He paused. "I... see."

Temper fled his face. She backed up as soon as her feet hit the concrete. Liam's jaw ticked, fingers curling into a fist.

"I'm sorry. The Bear is territorial. The scent is male, and mixed with your own. A father smells similar to a... lover sometimes."

She flushed, both hurt and angry. "You think I would cheat on you? If your nose is so good, then you should be able to smell that there aren't any sex scents in the apartment."

He grimaced, running a hand through his hair. "You're right, and as soon as you said it, common sense returned. I'm sorry, sweetheart." He studied her. "You're afraid of me now."

She shook her head. "Not really. My father had a temper when I was growing up. You startled me."

Liam tensed, eyes narrowing. "Does he hurt you?" He frowned. "You didn't tell me your father was staying with you."

Meredith thought quickly. "He came in town a little while ago. We don't have a good relationship and I didn't really want to introduce you two unless I knew we were serious, and even then..." she allowed her voice to trail off, lowering her eyes. Allowed discomfort and pain to show in her face. She wasn't lying, not exactly.

She felt him approach, his lips brushing her forehead. "I understand, sweetheart. If you want to come stay with me, you know you can, right?"

Meredith looked up, tempted.

He saw the look on her face and relaxed. "I bet there's better food at my house."

Meredith laughed. "I'll bet there is. But... Dad needs me right now. I'm trying to help him get on his feet. It'll help me in the long run if I help him now. He should be gone in a few days. Hopefully."

"Alright. But if you need me, call, okay?" His eyes flashed. "And if he bothers you, I'll take care of it."

Meredith was certain he would. And she was certain, now, that it would end in bloodshed, and maybe not just Harvey's.

CHAPTER

10

She'd left her charger in his truck.

"Fu-udge," she said, flopping down on her couch in disgust. She stared at her laptop. Six hours of lessons to teach, four hours left on the battery. Darnit. No choice. She rose, texting Liam, hating that she had to bother him, expecting to have to chase him down at the restaurant. She chewed her lip, brow furrowing; dealing with an aggravated Bear in Chef mode wasn't her idea of fun.

:Don't worry, sweet. I'll have my brother deliver.:

She sighed in relief. He wasn't annoyed, and she'd get her charger. The doorbell rang twenty minutes later. Meredith opened the door, staring at the male standing with her charger dangling from his hands.

"Hi," she said, head titling.

The man grinned. "I'm the handsome one."

Meredith smothered a snort. "Thank your mama," she said, reaching out. Frowning when he pulled the charger out of her reach, almost... teasing.

"I can see why he's besotted," Liam's brother said, gaze roaming up and down her body.

His eyes were chocolate rather than bottomless coal, hair with hints of red in the light rather than Liam's dense raven wing black. They were of a similar height, though this one seemed leaner, less intense. His eyes sparkled, mischievous in a bad boy trickster way that before meeting Liam, would have made heart patter- right before she backed away and slammed the door. Bad boys were so not her thing.

Even two weeks ago the presence of a strange male at her door would have disturbed her. She supposed something about belonging to Liam infused her with a new confidence. She didn't feel quite so alone anymore. Oh, she'd always had her mother, had Tamar. But this was different. Still, she resented this man's perusal and nearly slammed the door in his face. She *would* have words with Liam over his brother's manners.

"I hardly think he's besotted. Can I have my charger, please?"

He quirked an eyebrow. "If you give me a kiss."

Meredith's lips thinned. She began to close the door when he exclaimed.

"Okay, okay, just kidding."

She stopped. "I didn't think it was funny," she replied, voice flat.

He sighed. "He gets all the hot ones," he complained. "Listen, if you ever decide to leave that autocrat, I'm right here waiting, baby."

The... boy... opened his arms wide. Meredith shook her head, snatching the charger out of his hand, relaxing. He was just one big flirt with younger brother syndrome.

"I'll let Liam know you tried to poach on his woman," she said, shutting the door in his suddenly alarmed face.

Meredith rose from her crouch, craving one of Liam's cayenne mint lemonades, about to turn on her heels to go to the kitchen and ransack the pantry for at least the powdered stuff she kept on hand for the teens when she stumbled, dizziness momentarily blackening her vision.

A slender hand wrapped around her arm. "Whoa, teach. You okay?"

She waited until she could see again, a fine tremble in her knees, and realized the creeping fatigue she'd blamed on thirst and heat could be something more serious. She hadn't been able to eat that morning, appetite gone.

"I'm okay. Is Patrick still sick with the flu?" One of her teenagers had been missing for two days now, ever since the incident with Liam's brother, though he'd texted Meredith to let her know he would be back when he felt better. She'd appreciated the notice since they were getting to the time of year where every hand counted. There was canning to do, preserves and jams and salsa to make and package. Orders to fill from people who would come to the Farmer's Market to pick up their produce.

"He wasn't in school today," Brick said. "You didn't catch it did you?"

"I might have." It would explain the lingering touch of nausea for the last few days. "I'm going to go inside and sit down for a minute." And hope the crews were on a break and she could have some silence. Watching them convert the building into a culinary school with a small television studio was interesting, but noisy.

But by the day after next, Meredith realized she wasn't going to beat the virus after all. She woke up by the skin of her teeth, the kind of exhausted where it hurt to even lift her hand to fumble a text to Sheane. There was no way she was coming in today. She used her phone to go into her class schedule and canceled all her students for the next two days, to be on the safe side. Then allowed herself to sink back into sleep.

Pounding on the front door woke her, and the insistent vibrating of the cell where she'd dropped it next to her pillow. Meredith lifted her head, saw it was Liam, and came to a conclusion.

By the light coming through the curtains she knew it was well past afternoon. Sitting up, she realized she felt much better- since she could sit up without her head swirling and her body protesting the effort. Grimacing at the taste in her mouth, she texted Liam to give her five minutes to brush her teeth- they weren't quite at the stage where she was comfortable with bad breath and gunk in her eyes though they'd been together for over a month. The pounding stopped, but she could almost feel his hulking impatience.

"I'm coming," she muttered, doing nothing more than the bare minimum. She sniffed under her arm and winced. She'd let him in, then dash back to the bathroom and clean up for real. He'd just have to wait.

"Are you okay?" he demanded, walking in almost before she had the door open. She shuffled back quickly to avoid jamming her toes.

"The flu," she said.

"Sheane told me you were sick. Brick said it started two days ago. Why didn't you call me?"

She stared at him. "You were out of town. What do you think you were going to-"

He inhaled, nostrils flaring. "You smell different," he said, frowning.

"Well, Jesus, I would have taken a shower if you'd given me some warning."

"No. It's not that." He stared at her, a queer expression on his face. "Hey, I've got to make a phone call. I'll be right back, okay?"

Meredith shrugged. Whatever. It would give her time to wash up. By the time he returned she was clean, though her hair was still wet. She'd even slathered up in some of her favorite Bath and Body Works scented lotion,

215

the kind she always stocked up on but never had a reason to wear.

"That stuff is strong," Liam said, coming through the front door. "But not strong enough. Meredith, I need you to come with me."

"Where?" she asked. She'd just been about to make herself a sandwich, suddenly ravenous, and a cup of extra strong coffee to chase away the last vestiges of fatigue. "I was going to make a sandwich, I'm kinda hungry."

"You haven't eaten anything today?" His brow furrowed.

"Not in the last few days, really. I haven't had an appetite."

"Meredith! You have to eat." He grabbed her upper arm, hustling her out of the door. "We'll stop by the restaurant and get you something healthy. And you'll eat all of it."

"Oookaaay." She looked at him sideways, brow rising. "You're acting really weird. I'm not a skinny gal, you know. I won't waste away if I don't eat for a day or two."

His mouth firmed as he ushered her into the car, fastening her seatbelt with a fussiness that would have amused her if she weren't already annoyed. The restaurant wasn't far, or said annoyance would have gotten the better of her manners. He didn't seem in the mood to talk, so she closed her eyes and dozed the few minutes to his restaurant.

"I asked Mother to meet us here," Liam said, touching her shoulder.

Her eyes flew open as it hit her. "I'm meeting your mother?"

"Yeah. Don't worry about it."

He walked around the truck and opened her door, helping her down the step as if she were a fragile old woman.

"Liam, are you sure-"

"There's a nice rock eye salmon today," he said, ignoring her. "And a couscous cake we're working on with a dried berry compote. Sit down and I'll bring you a plate."

She felt odd, sitting down in the restaurant like a patron when she was the owner's girlfriend getting special treatment. Relaxed when he led her through the kitchen and into the back of the restaurant where there was an employee break room. It was nice, the walls painted in bistro neutrals. A flat screened television and the same tables and chairs from the restaurant were arranged comfortably. Employee lockers lined one wall, nice ones that weren't an eyesore with the decor.

"Sit down and I'll bring you a plate."

She sat and a few minutes later a tall young woman with a long dark braid and wide set hazel brown eyes entered the room with a steaming plate of food.

"Hi," she said, staring at Meredith.

Meredith stared back. After a second the woman moved, placing the food down on the table. Her head titled, nostrils flaring. She backed up several feet, eyes narrowing.

"Uh... hello." Meredith knew the woman must work in the kitchen- she wore a white jacket.

"I'm Norelle. Liam's sister."

Of course. She looked like Liam, albeit smaller and female, her features more delicate. She would have been very young at the time of the murder.

The female Bear shifted. "Liam asked me to bring that to you, he got caught up with a line cook. He'll be right back, though."

"Tell him to take his time," Meredith said, remembering to breathe.

The woman nodded and backed out of the room. Meredith began to eat a minute later, digging into the meal with two days' worth of hunger. She was half way through her meal and starting to feel full enough to look around for the television remote, when a door she hadn't noticed on the far side of the room buzzed. She stared, wondering what she should do. It buzzed again.

Rising, she opened the door. A young man in jeans and a branded polo stood at the door with a clipboard. "Delivery."

"Oh- um, I don't work here. Let me get someone."

She stuck her head out of the breakroom door and immediately winced.

"It's burnt," Liam roared. "And bland. Fire again, and this time get it right. Salt and pepper, salt and pepper!"

Meredith trotted down the hall and stopped at the kitchen threshold, not ashamed to admit to herself she felt somewhat.... intimidated. Norelle moved with whiplash speed as Liam barked orders, sleeves rolled up. He wasn't in a jacket, which told Meredith he hadn't planned on working.

"Liam?" she called, clasping her hands behind her.

His glanced her way, eyes narrow. She forced her feet to remain glued to the floor. "There's a delivery at the back door."

Norelle swore. "The market order. Kriss called off, she was supposed to handle that. I'll go."

"I need you on the line," Liam snapped, looking around.

"I can do it," Meredith said. "Just count all the boxes and make sure the order is correct, right? I help my mom out at her diner."

"You can judge produce?" Liam asked, frowning.

"Weelll, I grow it, so I think-"

He nodded, turning back to the line with a wave. "Go."

Feeling annoyance from his curtness would be a waste of emotional energy. Liam the Chef didn't care if she was aggravated by his brisk manner. He just wanted the job done.

Meredith went back to the break room, opening the door for the delivery man again. "I'll take care of everything. The kitchen is busy."

He looked her up and down with a raised brow but shrugged. "New intern?" he asked, waving a hand at his crew. Two men jumped out of the truck.

"Nah. Owner's girlfriend." It felt both odd and right to say it.

"Huh. Free food, man. I hear the chow here is good."

"It sure is." She took the clipboard and began marking off items, rifling through the boxes to inspect the fresh produce. Nothing canned, which she heartily approved of.

"Mere?"

Her head jerked up. "Dad?"

Harvey set a box on the ground, grinning. He wore a cap and the same branded polo. "Hey, small world."

"This is your new job?" She hadn't quite trusted him when he'd said he was working, trying to put his life back together.

"Yeah." He returned to the truck and unloaded another box. "They hire people with records. I didn't know you worked here."

"I don't," she replied quietly. "It's... my boyfriend does. I'm helping him out."

"Really? He's the manager?"

"Something like that."

"That's nice, sweetheart. Well, I've got to get back, I'll talk to you later, okay?"

She nodded, about to finish checking the last box when the back door swung open. Norelle stuck her head out.

"Hey, there was a lull, finally. Everything good?" The woman glanced at Harvey, and froze. "I know you," she said softly.

He glanced at her curiously. "Probably not. I've got an average kind of face. Hey, see you later, sweetheart, have a good day."

"You, too." It was stupid, she knew, but in that one moment the contentment in his normally shadowed eyes touched her heart and she couldn't bring herself to rebuff him. People could change, after all, and wasn't the point of jail to serve out a sentence? Who was she to continue to punish him - and herself- once society decided his sentence was over?

"You know him?" Norelle asked,

Meredith handed her the clipboard, brushing past her. "I was able to verify the order and everything looks good, but you'll want to double check. Tell Liam I had to get to the Y, okay?"

"Wait a minute," her lover's sister began, voice deepening.

"Bye," Meredith said brightly with a bouncy wave, walking fast through the alley and around to the front of the building. She'd just hop on a bus and get the hell out of there before Norelle put two and two together and told Liam.

But in her heart she knew she couldn't put off having that talk with him any longer.

CHAPTER

11

She hopped off the bus five blocks from her apartment to pick up a few items at the local drugstore. She knew she needed toilet paper, and Liam enjoyed popcorn so she would buy a jar of the old fashioned kind and look up recipes to make him something special. Maybe parmesan and cayenne for savory and a cinnamon brown sugar for sweet. She wasn't rich, but she tried to make up for it with little things.

Walking down the feminine products aisle, a bright pink box caught her eye. Rows and rows of pregnancy tests next to sanitary napkins. Mentally going through the contents of her drawers, she realized she hadn't touched the new pack she'd bought a little over a week ago to prepare for her clockwork cycle.

Meredith stopped, staring at the pads, eyes traveling from the plastic wrapped packages to the rectangular boxes. Her heartbeat jackknifed. She pulled her cell out to double-check dates. Remembered that she'd meant to schedule an appointment with the local clinic to renew her birth control prescription. She'd let it lapse over a year ago when it was obvious she'd lost interest in dating. There wasn't much to choose from in a town this size, especially when a good chunk of the eligible men were Bears, and until now she'd never imagined getting together with one of them.

Rapidly reading the claims on different boxes, she chose one that said it could detect a positive almost a week before a cycle was due. She was overdue- but maybe stress, or her crummy diet had affected things. Or maybe her dates were wrong. After that first initial encounter, they'd used protection. It took more than one time, didn't it?

Were Bears and humans even reproductively compatible?

She bought a buy one get one free pack just in case and hurried home, sipping a water bottle on the way. Meredith knew she'd have to pee on the stick. She knew that much, at least. Entering her apartment, she dropped her purse, not stopping to even catch her breath as she went to the bathroom. Tearing open the box, she sat on the side of the tub as she read through the instructions. It seemed cut and dry. It said results were more accurate first thing in the morning... but there was no way she could wait.

Meredith saturated the stick, wanting to laugh at herself over how carefully she approached the process of peeing on the bit of plastic. Wanted to laugh, but didn't. She places the test on the empty box and washed her hands then sat down to wait, swiping through junk mail on her cell to pass the longest few minutes of her life. When she couldn't take it anymore, she reached for the stick, flipping the box over at the same time to use the picture for comparison.

Stared at the picture. Stared at the box. Slid the test back into its white plastic covering and went to the kitchen to find a baggy to put it in.

She'd need proof when she told Liam she was pregnant.

Pregnant.

Worry, fear, and love blended; a tangle of weeds and wildflowers. Meredith couldn't separate one from the other. A baby. Could she even afford a baby, knowing how stressful it was to be a single mother? Mother and Tamar would offer support. It wasn't as if she were alone in the world, just... poor. Proper planning might alleviate strapped; extra hours at the diner, more students, writing that book she'd always wanted to write- even getting insurance through the state.

But through the positive self-talk her stomach curdled. Liam's baby. Liam's... cub. Would the baby be a Bear? Would it shift? The best action would be to talk to him right away... but she just couldn't, needing time to think, to digest, to come to some decisions on her own so she came to him with an idea of what she wanted already.

Meredith drove to Tamar's bar. She would be there since she worked the mid shift this day of the week, and Meredith could take a seat like usual and hang out with her when it was slow or she had a break.

It wasn't one of the busier days. The music was muted, only a quarter of the pool tables occupied. Meredith slid onto a stool at the bar, setting her purse on the counter.

Alphonso was working the bar. He approached from the far side, his long hair pulled back in a tail.

"Meredith. Did you want a drink or are you here to distract Tamar?"

She snorted. Charming, as usual. She hadn't noticed before because he was just Tamar's surly boss who made great cocktails, but now that she knew he was friends with Liam she paid more attention to him.

"I'll have a Sprite and wait till she's on break."

"A Sprite? That's not what you usually drink." He stopped talking. Leaned forward and.... sniffed her.

"Hey!" she exclaimed. "What is with all of you Bears today? Every Bear I've seen today has acted like I stink or something."

His expression didn't shift, and he didn't pull away. "Who else sniffed you?"

She frowned at him. "Liam, and his sister."

"Norelle. Did either of them... say anything?"

"What is going on? What exactly would they-" Meredith froze. Bears. Sniffing her. Liam, who could smell her father's scent in her apartment hours after he'd left, and tell it was laced with her own.

"Oh," she breathed. "Oh. My." She would bet her coffee money for a week that they had, somehow smelled maybe- a change in hormones?- something that indicated she was pregnant. Why else would Liam want her to talk to his mother all of a sudden? She swallowed.

"Can Bears smell... changes... in people? Physical changes?"

He pulled away finally. "I think you should go talk to Liam."

"Where's Tamar?"

He stared at her, expression stony, then jerked his head. "Doing side work. I'll get her."

That was a first. Her being pregnant must be a shock if Alphonso was fetching Tamar for her. It wasn't in character.

"Hey, girl. Al said you're looking for me. What's up?"

Meredith turned on her stool just in time to see the look Tamar gave Alphonso while his back was turned, walking around the counter again.

"Can you talk for a minute?"

Tamar glanced at her boss. "Yeah. He said to, actually. Weirdest thing. Come on, the stockroom is pretty quiet."

There were trays of tiny plastic salt and pepper shakers in the shape of

235

Bears lining several trays, a big box
each of salt and pepper and a funnel.

"This *is* Al's idea of a break," Tamar
said, sitting down. "Here."

"I haven't done this since junior
college," Meredith said. Glad to have
something her fingers could do.

"How's it going with Liam?"

"Funny you should ask." She
poured pepper into a tiny bear.
Paused, leaned forward and inhaled.
"Oh my God, that smells so good." She
inhaled the black pepper again, careful
not to get any in her nose. It was the
most fragrant smell ever, and she had a
sudden craving for French fries coated
in black pepper.

Tamar stared at her, looked at the
black pepper. "You're pregnant."

Meredith blinked, straightening
up. "How-"

"Are you kidding me? You're sniffing black pepper like it's chocolate brownies. I've never even seen you put it on food."

Meredith brow furrowed. "Huh. That's... weird."

"It's Liam's?"

She didn't know if she should feel insulted. She glared at Tamar. "Of course the baby is Liam's. What do you take me for?"

"Chill. Mixed species couples are rare."

Television movies did a wonderful job glamorizing strong Alpha Bear males and spinning fantastical tales of love with human women.

"I'm sure it's happened before," she said, hedging. Her worry spiked a notch, hand moving to her stomach.

"Are there even OBGYN's for mixed species pregnancies?"

"I wonder how big the babies get? Mine was nine pounds and 22 inches."

"Yeah, but she's a human baby, so it doesn't count."

Tamar continued to fill shakers, eyes on her work. "Hmm. When are you going to tell him?" She looked up. "You're keeping the baby, right?"

Meredith didn't say anything, brows furrowed.

"Meredith!"

"Yes, I'm keeping the baby, I just-what if he doesn't want to co-parent?"

"Then you do it on your own. Your mom will help. And Andra will have a playmate near her age."

Tears pricked. "I'm going to go see him now. I have to get it over with so I can move on with whatever I need to do."

Tamar nodded approvingly, reaching out a hand to squeeze Meredith's hand. "That's right. And then take a vitamin, buy a book to read and get some rest. Trust me- everything will normalize soon."

Meredith saw several missed calls and a text from Liam. She texted him back, letting him know she was waiting for him at his place and to take his time. He replied a few minutes later.

:Norelle just took off. Stuck here. Key under mat. Squeeze some orange juice.:

The instruction warmed her. She was nearly convinced now that Liam already knew she was pregnant. Him wanting to take care of her health- even if it was just for the baby- was a good sign he was planning on sticking around.

She couldn't quite let herself in his house, though, even though the cat was kinda out of the bag. Instead, she sat on the porch, killing time by scrolling through Amazon for books on pregnancy, downloading a few frees and one or two paids that had good reviews. Because reviews were everything, which was why she always tried to leave an honest review if she liked a book because she knew it helped the author.

The sound of a car door slamming caught her attention. She looked up, surprised to see Norelle fast walking up the sidewalk, expression tight. Meredith stood, setting her cell down.

"Norelle? Is everything okay?" She didn't know the woman, but she was Liam's sister so that was enough for Meredith to feel some genuine concern. Plus, she would be the baby's aunt as well.

Dark eyes, so like Liam's, gleamed with fury. Clenched fists and swelling shoulders clued Meredith in a second before the woman spoke. She took a step away from Norelle, then stopped, bracing herself, a suspicion in her stomach that her... omission... was about to come out into the light.

CHAPTER

1 2

"You lying bitch."

Meredith reacted instinctively as
the blur of a human hand morphing into
a paw sheathed in glossy dark fur
swung towards her in an arc she barely
saw. She flung her arms up in front of
her face just in time to absorb the

sudden impact of the fall as she hurtled backward. Her head banged against the porch and she thought, distantly, that she would have matching bruises on her head and forearm.

Anger surged. "I didn't lie. I tried to tell him, but he didn't want to listen."

"You didn't try hard enough." Norelle's shoulders seemed to swell, shirt tightening around her curvy form. "He's in love with you- in love with the daughter of the man who killed our father."

Meredith closed her eyes, squeezing the lids against tears. What could she say? Norelle wasn't saying anything unfair. "I'm sorry," she whispered. "It was my fault." She opened her eyes, jaw clenching. "But if you swing on me again- I'll take you out." She wouldn't allow anyone to hit her- not for any reason.

Norelle's scorn seared. "No, that wasn't your fault. But breaking my brother's heart *is*. And I'll be damned if I let you do it."

"Norelle."

An older female voice lashed out, halting the continued threat of the angry young woman.

"Mother-"

"Go to the cabin and stay there until I come for you."

There was no going against the steel in that voice. Meredith would rather be hit again than face the person behind the whiplash. She rose to her feet, forcing herself to face more werebear music. Meredith looked into the face of an older Norelle. A female Liam.

Oh, shiii-oot. "You're his Mother?"

Eyes a shade between Liam's coal and Boden's deep umber regarded her. "His mother, Gwenafar, and head of the Mother's Council."

Meredith heard the capitalization of the name. "What is that?"

"Come, Liam wanted you to drink a glass of juice. We're the ones who told the Alpha's to find human brides."

"Wait- what?"

Meredith stopped, heels digging into the wood as the woman bent and took the key from under the mat. "Liam was told to find a human woman to... marry?"

"Yes, and he's an obedient son, even if he didn't like the idea at first."

Her stomach churned. He was courting her because he *had* to? Because his mother said so?

"Don't get any ideas," Gwenafar said. "He's courting you because he wants to, not because I told him to. And no, I'm not reading your mind. Your face is very expressive."

Meredith lifted a hand to the back of her head, absently. It throbbed, pain increasing now that she was paying attention to it. Her fingers came away sticky. She stared at her hand.

"Oh."

Gwenafar sighed. "I don't smell much blood, but I have first aid supplies in my truck. You learn to carry them with children like mine. Go sit in the kitchen and I'll be right back."

She didn't have much of a choice. The woman's dominance wrapped around her, insidious in a way even Liam couldn't manage. Gwenafar's presence reminded Meredith of her mother, her Grandmother, her Sunday school teacher and every other female figure of authority and comfort she'd ever know rolled into one. It confused her, put her off balance. All she knew was she wanted to please this woman with obedience.

Gwenafar glanced at her when she came back in the house, setting a clear plastic box on the island. "You feel the matrilineal bond, don't you? I imagine it's uncomfortable since you're not used to it." She paused. "But then, my daughter hates it, too."

"I- you mean I'm picking up on some kind of werebear thingy? How is that possible?"

"I would guess because you and Liam have become... close."

Meredith blushed, staring straight ahead. She never imagined she'd be having a conversation about her and Liam's sex life with his *mother*.

"He hasn't mated you- we would all know. And there are formalities to observe because he is our Alpha. But it isn't from lack of pressure from his Bear."

"I think we should get to know each other better before we make any long term decisions," Meredith replied quietly.

"Hmm. Wise. But he can only hold off the Bear for so long. The longer you are in each other's presence, the tighter the ropes that bind. That he's held off this long is admirable. I always did think it better to delay a mating as long as possible to give the human halves time to come to terms."

Mating? Bonds? Oh, Liam was in so much trouble. If he had the nerve to be angry at her for keeping secrets....

"I'll get that scrape cleaned as best I can. Your hair is in the way so no bandages, but I think- ah. Yes, not too bad. It's already beginning to heal."

Gwenafar sounded pleased. "This is going to be a very strong mating. It's what we need for our Alpha, and the Den."

It stung a little, her ministrations, though Meredith could tell the woman was trying to be as gentle as possible. "Why was Liam asked to marry a human woman?"

Gwenafar sighed. "It's purely practical. Our communities are too small and most of the young couples are related in some way or another. We need new genes in the pool or we'll die out."

Meredith blinked. "Uh- genes? You mean you want human women to..."

"Have cubs? Yes. As many as possible. Female preferably." Gwenafar leveled her with a stern look. "You're playing a very important role to my people, Meredith. You should admire

Liam for making what could have been a serious sacrifice in a different situation."

"I do admire him." That was the problem. In the last few weeks he'd shown himself to be kind, humorous, fierce. Protective. Stubborn and growly and autocratic, but she supposed he couldn't help it.

"I let myself think we were going to have a future," Meredith said to herself.

"You *are* going to have a future."

Meredith into kind, but implacable, eyes. "You know who I am."

"Yes, I do. And it doesn't matter." Gwenafar paused. "Or rather, it shouldn't matter. Your father's actions are not your own."

And she finally accepted that. Meredith didn't know at what point she'd come to understand she wasn't to blame for Harvey. Maybe the time spent with Liam, ironically. Who was open and understanding. Gentle, reining in the frequent flashes of temper she knew he unleased with impunity on his staff.

"I don't want to tell him." Meredith laughed. "It's ironic. I kept trying to tell him, and he didn't want to listen. And now I don't want to tell him, but I'm sure Norelle is going to, so I have to beat her to it."

"Norelle will keep her mouth shut. If you want to tell him- go ahead. If you don't, then don't. My son isn't stupid and although this is a painful secret, I'm much more interested in my future grandchildren than I am in his issues with forgiveness. I forgave Harvey a long time ago, Meredith. I had to, in order to move on. Liam needs to let go as well."

Meredith just hoped the process didn't destroy their chance for a family.

She wasn't ready to face Liam. Meredith figured the best way to duck a Bear with a nose in a town this size was to go to Tamar's house. She was sure Liam didn't know where her best friend lived, and the house was far enough outside city limits that it would take more than the typical five to ten minute in town drive to get there.

They made dinner- well, Tamar did most of the cooking while Meredith played with the baby. She picked her up and went to the nursery, a charming room her industrious mother designed to mimic a magazine cover. Only this room was designed using dollar and thrift store finds. Looking at the framed letters, pretty hand sewn bedding and small touches here and here, Meredith couldn't tell the difference. It gave her hope that raising a child on a limited income was possible. Though, if she sat down and thought, she had to smack herself on the forehead. Looking back, she realized that even though her mother had never complained about money, it must have been tight. Father in jail, Mom working sometimes two jobs. But their home- especially, ironically- after Dad was gone was always clean, always cheerful. Meredith never felt poor, especially since she was a natural DIY'er.

She wondered how many of the fun weekend projects were because Mom just hadn't had the money for new and fancy.

Meredith busied herself by playing dress up with baby, taking care to hang up the frilly little skirts and dresses when she was done parading baby around and snapping pics on the cell. Tamar poked her head in the door, saw what was going on and snorted.

"Divas, dinner is ready."

Meredith picked baby up. "Come, sweetbee, time to eat. And let's put on this pretty little bibby so baby don't get her little dressy all messy."

And she was glad she'd put the bib on, feeding baby a bottle of breastmilk while her mother enjoyed eating her dinner slowly for a change. Meredith was happy to give Tamar a small break- especially since she fully intend to swipe a big piece to take home for lunch tomorrow. The woman could cook. Meredith realized she was going to have to brush up on her skills as well. She defaulted to chicken and veggie stir fry or salad or tuna little too often.

The doorbell rang, a halfhearted buzz that ended in a low drone as the visitor continued to punch it.

Tamar frowned. "Who the hell could that be?"

There was a clear line of sight from the kitchen to the open living room so Meredith watched curiously as Tamar opened the door. Stared.

"How the hell do you know where I live?" the woman demanded.

"Is she here?" a deep male voice growled.

Meredith's eyebrows shot up. It sounded like-

"I can smell her." He pushed his way into the house.

-Alphonso.

"Hey! You can't come in here!"

Meredith rose, picking up the baby, wary from the sudden fury and alarm in Tamar's voice. Something was wrong hand it activated every instinct inside her. Her lip curled back, a growl escaping her chest as she folded her arms around the toddler.

Alphonso stopped short, staring at her. Tamar hurried after him, also staring when she saw Meredith.

"Mere?"

"Danger," she said, guttural. A flood of protective fury rose and she backed away from Alphonso.

"Meredith-"

Tamar began to walk towards her, but Alphonso grabbed the woman's wrist. "Be still. She's just reacting to the alarm in your voice. Stay calm and it will go away." He assessed Meredith. "I'm not going to hurt the baby. Liam is looking for you." He inhaled. "You're reacting like a Bear female- interesting. I know he didn't bite you. Must be the pregnancy. That's a good thing- means the baby inside you will be a strong Bear. Are you eating enough? You'll need more calories, and meat, to keep your energy up. Why don't you give Tamar the baby so you can sit down and finish your dinner?"

He continued to ramble in a low, monotone Meredith found soothing. Her expression softened, shoulders drooping as she began to feel normal again.

She blinked. "Oh. Um, yes. Baby should finish eating, too."

Tamar approached, wary but calm, and took her daughter, sitting her back in her seat.

"Come on, Mere, you should eat."

She may have been calm, but a vein of tension still ran through the other woman, who refused to look at Alphonso. Meredith looked at her, head cocked, wondering what was wrong.

"Al, you delivered your message, you should go now."

He nodded, began to turn away and glanced at the baby again. "Cute kid. The lasagna smells good, too. Might have to put you on kitchen-"

Alphonso froze, turned back around, eyes bright as his attention latched onto the child. Tamar rose immediately, picking the baby back up.

"Leave, Alphonso," she snapped. "I have to get ready for work tomorrow and you're bothering me."

He took a step towards them, staring at the child. He inhaled again, a long and deliberate breath. Tamar began to back away, turning as he approached. Stalked.

"You can't run," he said, a hoarse whisper as if he were trying to keep from roaring. Meredith stood back up, about to speak. His head snapped towards her, fangs flashing a warning. Even a week ago she would have stumbled back, but whatever predator hormones were flooding her system reared to the surface with a vengeance. She snarled back with her human teeth, body feeling as if there was a beast trying to get out.

"Jesus! You two stop!" Tamar yelled. The baby began to growl, tiny high pitched rumbles as she kicked in her mother's arms.

Meredith was shocked out of anger, staring at the child.

"That's right, little Bear," Alphonso murmured, satisfaction glinting in his eyes. "Strong." His face hardened as he looked at an ashen Tamar. "How long did you think you could keep her from me?"

"Wait- what?" Meredith was floored. The implication- she looked at

Tamar, and knew the implication was more than that. Was truth.

"Oh. My. God. I thought you said the daddy was this white guy in Seattle."

"I'm the white guy from Seattle," Alphonso replied, dry as dragon's breath. "Though I take exception to the 'white.'" He looked at Meredith, expression flat. "Liam is trying to reach you. I told him you'd be here."

She folded her arms. "I don't want to talk to him."

"He is Alpha. You will not defy him. Go now, or I'll take you myself."

"Hey, you can't talk to her like that," Tamar interjected.

Alphonso smiled at her. His fangs had not receded. "We have talking to do, woman. I'd suggest you take a seat. *Go*, Meredith."

CHAPTER

13

The hormones that gave her courage to confront Alphonso must have spurred her on to meet Liam even though a part of her wanted to find the darkest movie theater and hang out for a few days. He knew she was pregnant; he knew his baby was the grandson of the man who had killed his father.

Meredith didn't know how any man could handle that kind of doozy without snapping. She just hoped it wasn't their relationship that was going to give- and braced herself for the worst.

It was late by the time she pulled up outside Liam's house. She sat in her car, leaning back in the seat with her eyes closed for several minutes. Trying to gather energy for the coming... discussion. It wasn't until the car door opened that she realized she'd fallen asleep.

Meredith blinked, lids flying open as the sudden movement startled her into wakefulness. She managed to squelch her yelp of surprise and gave her heart a few beats to settle back in her chest. Until she saw the look on Liam's face, and it started up again.

Or the lack of look.

Liam turned, leaving the door open, and walked toward the house.

Meredith emerged slowly, fussing with the lock, stalling. He paused at his front door, waiting for her to catch up.

"I don't think I need to come in," she said, shifting. "Um... this talk won't take long. I mean- it's late and I don't want to keep you-"

He looked at her, hand on the knob. Meredith shut her mouth, proceeding him into the house. He took her arm, leading her to the kitchen and putting her on a stool like a toddler. Meredith frowned. When he placed a sandwich and glass of milk in front of her, she stared at the plate.

"Alphonso said he interrupted your dinner," Liam said. His voice was different, devoid of its usual warmth.

"I'm not really hungry."

A brownie slid under her nose, right next to the sandwich. Eyeing the thick square of fudge, Meredith's hand edged toward the treat when it was yanked away. She gasped, head jerking up to glare at Liam.

Dark eyes implacable, he said, "Sandwich first. Brownie second."

The sandwich disappeared one resentful bite at a time, more to avoid wasting the food than for any other reason. Liam could afford wasted food, but that wasn't the point. The silence was becoming oppressive. She didn't know whether to be uncomfortable or angry at this kind of passive aggressive temper.

"You lied to me," he said when she was done eating, words inflectionless.

"Not really. I tried to tell you, but you said-"

"I know what I said."

Meredith tried to put herself in his shoes. Her growing anger softened almost immediately- she didn't feel guilty anymore for Harvey, but she could still feel compassion for the son who'd lost his father.

"I'm sorry, Liam," Meredith said, staring at her plate. "I've felt guilty for years because of what my Dad did. I felt it was my fault." She swallowed. "That day- he and Mom were arguing about the farm. They couldn't afford the payments and the bank told him it was being bought by Kyle Conroy. And there was a new pair of shoes I wanted." She tried to smile. "Disney Princess. I was so mad that I couldn't get my shoes, and I blamed him, and I blamed your Dad. And he just looked at me, then he took the shotgun and left. The look on my mother's face... I don't know if she knew. We haven't talked about it."

It hit her then, that her baby would never know its grandfather who by all accounts had been a good man and a good Alpha.

"I'm sorry." Tears pricked her eyes. "I should go."

She started to rise, blinking rapidly. "Sit down," Liam said, icy. The tears began to gather in earnest, spilling down her cheeks. He swore, muttering under his breath.

"It's not the baby," she said, trying to muffle her crying in her hands. "I feel so bad."

She felt the heat of his body and then arms swinging her up against a broad chest. He walked out of the kitchen, taking her to the living room where he sat down on the couch, cradling her.

"I'm handling it," he said. "You don't have to cry. I know it's not your fault. It's just a shitty coincidence. Where is he?"

She sniffed, swiping her arm over her eyes. "He moved into a place, got a job."

"Yeah. Norelle told me. I had to hear this from *Norelle.* She's kicking up a fuss with the entire Den." He swore, viciously, arms tightening aground Meredith. "Damnit, Meredith. If you'd told me I could have been prepared to deal with the fallout."

She glared up at him. "You said that unless I was an ax murderer you didn't care what my family had done!"

He grimaced. "I'll never do that again, I promise. Is there anything else you should tell me?"

Her bottom lip poked out. She didn't appreciate the sarcasm. He was as much to blame as she was, but- he didn't seem mad, just distant and grim.

She could deal with that. Give him time and space and things would be alright.

"What about the baby?" she asked, plucking at his shirt. She lowered her eyes, not wanting to see disappointment or denial.

"Sweetheart, I'm ecstatic about the cub."

She took a deep breath, relief loosening some of the tension in her muscles "Are you going to ever talk to my Dad? We can't keep the baby away from him."

He stiffened against her, chest harder than granite. "That bastard isn't coming anywhere near my cub," he growled.

Meredith held back her response. But... they had at least nine months, and time after that as well, for him to come around. And push come to shove, she could just... figure something out when

Liam wasn't around. It was then she realized she'd forgiven her father. Otherwise she wouldn't have been concerned whether he saw the... cub. She rested her head on Liam's chest, listening to the steady beat of his heart, tired.

"I need to get home," she said.

"Is your laptop with you?"

"Yes. In the trunk."

"Then stay the night." His lips brushed the top of her head. "There's some things in the top drawer for you." Liam paused, sighed. "I'm not happy about this, Meredith- but it isn't the end of things. You're mine, and that isn't going to change because we encounter difficulty."

By 'this' she knew he meant her father, and not the pregnancy. "Okay."

He carried her to the room and set her on her feet, leaving her to wash up and crawl into the cal king bed, drawing the quilt u to her chin. She stayed awake for a while, listening for his footsteps. But he didn't come.

Liam knew he had to handle his emotions, keep them from bleeding out onto the innocent woman carrying his cub. Intellectually he understood she wasn't to blame for her father. She wasn't even to blame for wanting to keep it a secret- how could she not want to keep that secret? No one wanted to live with a dark shadow looming over her heads. She managed to make a life for herself, grow into a caring, feisty, independent woman.

So he would deal with his anger, his hatred. Bear brushed it off. Didn't care two fiddles for her sire, only cared about the woman, the cub. She must be taught not to lie, but her sire meant nothing in the long scheme of things. Life comes, life goes. It was the way of things.

But for now he had a more pressing issue.

Normally his duties as Alpha of a small town Den were mostly perfunctory. He helped keep the young males in check, maintained contact with local agencies, protected their private lands from government encroachment. They didn't delve much into politics in their territory- it was too small to bother with, mostly. But with the onset of the Mother's Council decisions to intervene in affairs of reproduction, life was more... complicated lately.

He left Meredith sleeping in his bed and slipped out of the house. The males gathered deep in the forest, restless and demanding reprieve. The

ten- well, nine, since one was missing-
who'd been chosen in the lottery
including himself were present. And
Alphonso, his second, though his name
hadn't been pulled. The canopy
overhead blanketed the clearing,
nearly blocking out light from the rising
sun. Their shifter eyes glowed, no trouble
piercing the dark.

Males turned as Liam
approached, took his place in the
center. He'd always thought it symbolic;
the circle could either be a protection-
or a vise.

He held up a hand, calling for
silence. "I know there are objections to
the decree and the results of the
lottery." He paused. "I don't like it any
more than you do, being forced to find
a human mate against my will. But. I've
done what is required of me."

"We know about your human," a male said. "And we know it has been no hardship for you to take her."

Boden had been running his mouth. "I got lucky," he agreed. "My Bear likes this woman. All that means is that if you stop whining and start looking, you can find a woman your Bear will want as well." He stared at them, expression hard. "Is the survival of our people not worth this small sacrifice? How many of you already have females?"

Silence. Liam smiled. "The Mother's aren't stupid. That's why our names were put in the lottery. Because none of us is entangled. Think of this as a war, and a human woman is your prisoner and your prize."

"And what are we supposed to do? How are we supposed to find women?"

Liam shrugged, irritated. "How do human males find women? Look on the internet. Ask around. Put an ad in the damn newspaper. But I'm giving you each a year to comply with the decree. And after a year, I will find you. And you will face me in the Challenge circle." Because if he had to go through with it, then damnit, they all had to go through with it.

They spoke, argued, for a while longer. The sun was just over the sky when Liam finally called a halt to the discussion. There was still disgruntlement- but most expressions reflected resignation, even eagerness. Evidently word on his woman had gotten around, and more than one male had already taken a peek at Meredith. There weren't that many fire haired, curvy beauties in town. If Liam was able to find a willing human so quickly, then they should be able to do the same.

"Liam."

His head jerked around in surprise. He stared at Norelle, displeased, eyebrow rising. "Norelle, what are you doing here? This was a meeting for the males only." They didn't invade the women's business. It was a serious breach of etiquette for her to invade theirs.

"I've been listening to this talk of mates, of human women." She stepped into the clearing. Voices fell, staring at the Alpha's sister. "Everyone congratulates you for being so self-sacrificing. But there is one problem."

Her lip pulled back in a snarl. Liam tensed. "The human woman he is planning to mate is the daughter of our family's enemy. The daughter of the man who killed our father."

The males looked between him and Norelle.

Alphonso stepped closer to him, abandoning his apparent nonchalance. "Go home, Norelle," he said, voice deceptively mild. "It's none of your concern."

"Shut up, Alphonso," she snapped. "You would go along with anything he did out of stupid male loyalty. Even let him foul our family line with that monster's git."

Liam gritted his teeth. He understood her anger, her pain, her sense of betrayal. But he couldn't allow her to insult Meredith. Not the mother of his cub.

"Norelle, Meredith is having my cub." Surprise rippled through the males. "I know this is difficult, but you have to accept it. I won't have you insulting her, or punishing your niece or nephew."

"I will never accept it. If you don't repudiate her-"

"You'll do what?" he growled, stepping forward. Sister or not- he wouldn't let her get away with threatening him.

Norelle's shoulders swelled. A sound of challenge burst from her throat. His Bear reacted, echoing the roar with one of his own.

He was Alpha because he was the strongest, his shift from man to Bear the fastest. The change ripped through him, bursting the seams of his clothing even as Norelle's shift matched his own in speed and strength. If she'd been a man, she would have Challenged him a long time ago to be Alpha. But she wasn't.

He rose on hind legs, meeting her charge, maw gaping. They collided, powerful arms each seeking purchase around the other. Liam held back, reluctant even with the fury of Bear roaring through his veins, to hurt his sister. She was smaller, lighter- but fast, and vicious in her anger. She swiped at him. He grabbed her around the shoulders, flinging her bodily into the ground. She twisted, gaining her feet and lunging even as he followed up with a tackle. Norelle's paw rammed into his head. She jumped on his back, teeth snapping. He threw her off and returned the favor, wrestling her to the ground with superior weight and strength, jaw sinking into her neck, demanding she surrender. She tried to break free and couldn't. He increased the pressure, enough to break through fur and skin, pressing down until she was flat on the ground, pinned.

He felt the ripple of her muscles as she began to shift back, defeated. Released her neck, backing away warily until he was certain it wasn't a trick, then rushed through his change to stand as a man again.

"Get her something to cover herself," he snapped at Alphonso.

The male took off his sleeveless black shirt, tossed it at Norelle who put it on. The males averted theirs eyes out of respect- or because Liam stared them down.

"Norelle, you're banished for thirty days," he said as she rose to her feet. "Go to New York, bring back Cassius." The male who hadn't been present, though he was one of the ten whose name's had been drawn. "But don't let me see you again before your banishment is done."

Someone muttered under their breath. Liam's head snapped towards the voice and he took a step. "Does someone have an opinion?" he roared. His blood boiled, anger seeking an outlet, incisors itching for something to sink into. Norelle had activated his Bear, but he'd held back, hadn't fully unleashed the lust for battle.

"Liam, go to Meredith before you start a fight," Alphonso said sharply.

Liam's nostrils flared, head swinging around in the direction of his home. Yes. Meredith. That was better than destroying another male. *Meredith.*

He didn't even think as he slid back into Bear, charging through the forest to get to his woman.

Alphonso supposed he should feel guilty for siccing Liam on Meredith, but the man needed an outlet and she was better than him injury one of the males. That would really piss the Mother's off. Besides, the Bear wouldn't hurt Meredith. Still, he supposed the woman at least deserved a heads up.

Shrugging, he took out his cell and called Gwenafar. She'd deal with it.

She texted him that morning, figuring he must have gone in to open the restaurant or oversee some work at the Y. Today was a garden day, so maybe she would see him there later. Her heart was only half way into her classes, but thankfully the lessons that had been preloaded were ones she was already familiar with so she could breeze through the activities with each student while her mind was half-way somewhere else.

It was after lunch when she'd checked her cell for the dozenth time and saw there were no missed calls or texts. Irritated, she angry texted and erased several messages just to get it out of her system. Set the phone down and went back to her laptop to check the lesson plan for her next student when her cell rang.

She snatched it up. "Liam?"

"Where are you?"

Meredith recognized the mature female voice; Gwenafar. "I'm at Liam's."

"Stay there. He's on his way."

Gwenafar hung up. Meredith wanted to text her back, worry pricked from the grim tone, but she opted for patience and cancelled the student, wincing from the ding it would put on her quality ranking for the month, and sat outside on the porch, oddly nervous.

A roar sounded from the forest across the street. The sound shook her to her bones and she pushed to her feet, mouth dry, breaths fast and shallow.

A giant brown Bear exploded from the tree line, leaves showering to the ground with the force of his passing. He stopped short when he saw Meredith, rearing up onto hind legs so he stood nearly ten feet tall. His maw gaped, white fangs gleaming.

"Liam," she whispered.

He fell forward onto four legs, porch trembling with the shock of his weight. Forward he walked, one lumbering step at a time, dark eyes pinning her to the spot.

She couldn't have moved if she'd wanted to. The intelligence, the warmth was gone, replaced by a fury of intermingles lust and anger. She didn't know how she knew that; if she closed her eyes she could almost feel the turmoil inside him.

When she forced her lids open, he was walking up the steps, the wood creaking under his weight even as his form began the reverse transition, muscles shrinking, fur receding. Face morphing into that of a human male- a naked human male, chest and shoulders sculpted with a strength she knew could crush her.

The Bear hadn't frightened her; seeing the huge, moist erection on the man as he stalked toward her, she stumbled back several feet.

"Liam-"

"Shut up," he snarled. He leaped from the bottom step, clearing the stair case and porch in one powerful thrust of his thighs, landing in front of her with a thud that rivaled an earthquake. She backed into house, banging her head with the force of her retreat.

"Ow," she exclaimed, rubbing the smarting skin. And began to get angry at him for scaring her. "Either you control your temper, or I'm leaving!" She refused to be with a man who thought it was okay to frighten her, or cause her any kind of injury, no matter how small.

Arms caged her on either side as he leaned into her, nose buried in her neck. Teeth sank into her soft flesh, just enough to make a point, not enough to hurt.

"Not going anywhere, Meredith."

Her voice trembled. "Are you going to make me?"

Silence stretched. He pulled away from her slowly, amber eyes still hot and growly, but giving her space. Choice. She took a deep breath, licking her lips. His eyes fastened on the movement and his chest swelled even further.

"Do you want to know the best way to handle an angry mate?" he asked softly.

Um... no? Yes? She watched him warily. "Okay. How?"

He smiled, sharp inhuman incisors gleaming. "Fuck him senseless."

Her clit pulsed. "You already have no sense," she muttered, glancing at the erection. She realized they were standing outside. "Liam, get inside!"

He folded his arms. "Make me."

She glared. "Everyone will see-" she waved a hand in his general direction, "-this."

He didn't move. Meredith stepped into him, hand wrapping around the twitching cock, squeezing. "Come inside, Liam," she demanded in a low, husky tone.

Reason left his face, smile evaporating as a shudder racked his body. He lifted her, throwing her over his shoulder and ramming through the front door. She could only see the floor- and his firm ass- but she knew he took her to the living room. A moment later he lowered her onto the pile of thick rugs in front of the fireplace. She figured she should be glad he hadn't just tossed her without regard for the landing.

Strong hands reached for the neck of her blouse, ripping cloth like butter. Buttons scattered as she squeaked. Her jeans and panties were next before he unsnapped the delicate lace bra. She spared a thought to have a moment of indignation- he didn't care about the plain white blouse, but he took care with the sexy lingerie. What a... male.

"Liam, what happened? Talk to me."

"I don't want to talk. I want my woman."

Her hands buried in his hair, holding his head still. He allowed it. "Either you tell me why your mother called me sounding weird-"

"My sister Challenged me."

Her mouth gaped. "Norelle? What? What does that mean?"

Liam stared down at her, eyes hard as resin chips. "She doesn't want me to mate you. Says it shames our father. Challenged me for rule of Den."

Meredith's eyes closed, dread in the pit of her stomach. She hadn't seen any blood on him, any injuries. Gwenafar hadn't sounded *too* perturbed...

"Is she alright?"

He smiled, and Meredith shivered. "She's learned a lesson. And no one in my Den will Challenge my right to rule- or my right to my mate, again."

She hesitated, eyes lowering. "Maybe she's right."

"Not right," he said with short, guttural syllables. "Lied to me. Enemy's daughter. But still my mate. Mine to punish."

Meredith stilled, unable to move as he wrapped long locks of her red hair around his fist, tightening to the point of discomfort.

"You said you didn't blame me," she whispered, not daring to cover her naked breasts, stung that he'd called her his enemy's daughter. Stung at the faintest hint of venom.

His eyes closed, shudder rippling through his body. The veins in his neck stood out in stark relief.

"Bear doesn't care. Man... struggling."

Meredith thought she understood. A Bear would understand the cycle of life and death, of predator and prey. The practicality of living in the wild precluded holding grudges when mating and the protection of kin was at stake. The Bear only cared that she was his, and carried his cub. The man wasn't nearly as practical.

"What do you want me to do?" she asked, waiting on his response. "Whatever you need from me to heal- I'll give it."

Not because she felt guilty, not because his dominance frightened her. But because she knew he was a good man, and because her actions had led to the life growing within her- a life that deserved the best possible chance to have a happy childhood with both parents.

He shifted, body collapsing to cover her, face burying in her neck.

"Just be you," he whispered against her skin, voice regaining its humanity from her acquiescence. "I won't give you up."

"You don't have to." Her hand dared to stroke his silk dark hair, stroke the bare skin of his back. The muscles tensed and he raised back up.

"But," he said, expression hard. Hot. "You need to be punished. Hard. And fast."

CHAPTER 14

Meredith struggled to contain a smug, wicked grin. Instead, she lowered her eyes, shrinking away from him with an instinctive feminine wile, hair falling over her face in a silky curtain of glossy red.

"Don't hurt me," she said, allowing a tremble in her voice, almost ruined by a husky note of anticipation. She didn't know how much longer she could play her part. She wanted him, was close to demanding he fuck her. But she also knew her pleasure would be greater the more dominant he felt. Submitting to him activated an electric thrill in her; she wasn't a weak woman for all her wariness of men. She wanted a strong man to take her, to fuck her- but a worthy strong man. Liam.

He pulled her up to her knees by her hair, still not quite painful, but borderline. Tears pricked her eyes and she gasped, hands catching her fall on his chest.

"Oh, Liam," she breathed, stifling a giggle, rubbing her soft breasts and belly against his hard torso, the shifter heat of his body nearly scalding. "Punish me. I lied to you- I deserve to be punished. I want to be punished."

He nodded, satisfied by her penitence. "Good. My mate must be honest, and obedient." He paused, eyebrow quirked, free hand stroking her cheek. "How are you going to show your regret?"

"I-" she licked her lips, hand traveling down his chest, hesitantly, as she peeked up through her lashes. Her fingers wrapped around his engorged cock, squeezing gently, caressing the length. "Let me put my mouth on you. I want to show how sorry I am."

Her clit throbbed, pussy dampening in response to her own words, in response to the vivid images racing through her mind. Her nipples hardened, breasts drawing up from the ache. His eyes lowered to her chest, flaring.

"Yes," he said softly. "I can see how much you want it. Lay down."

He released her hair as she stretched out on her back, reaching for him as he climbed up her body. He rose over her, a sculpted, dominant god of a man, wicked intent on his face. His cock bumped her lips, a stinging smack. She opened her mouth, accepting the silken girth, drawing him as deep as she could into her throat.

It was the first time she'd wanted to do this with a man, for a man. The first time her tongue eagerly swiped along the mushroom head of a cock, lips forming a perfect O as he began to fuck her mouth, hard and fast as she struggled to learn the rhythm.

She cupped his balls, massaging the sacs, a heady sense of power filling her as he moaned, head lolling back on his shoulders in ecstasy.

"Yes," he hissed. "Take all of me, baby. Fuck my cock with that hot little mouth."

Long fingers gripped her breasts, batting and playing, tugging her nipples until she groaned around his cock. Tasting salty pre-cum, their liquids mingling in her mouth. She swallowed the moisture to keep it from dribbling down her chin, yearning for him to do to her pussy what he was doing to her mouth.

"Are you sorry?" he asked hoarsely, pinching her nipple. She cried out, pain and pleasure startling her. "Are you sorry you lied?"

He pulled out of her mouth so she could speak. Meredith swallowed once. "Yes, Liam, I'm sorry. Please, I'm sorry. I won't lie to you again." Though if he punished her like this- maybe she would.

The Alpha stroked her hair. "I think you mean it. And because I'm almost convinced, I'll give you a reward." He moved away from her and she sat up.

"I'm going to fuck this tight pussy, Meredith, and then when I'm done, I'm going to put my cock in your ass. No part of you will be foreign to me; every part of your body will know I'm your Alpha." He paused. "Are you with me, Meredith? Am I your Alpha?"

She trembled, eager desire and terrible apprehension mingling in a heady cocktail. He could scent it, of course, his cock swelling even wider, dark red and throbbing.

"I'm with you," she said, shifting around onto her knees without him asking.

His hand pressed her shoulders, pushing her torso to the bed so her plump ass rose in the air. Spreading her thighs wide apart, she felt the tip of his cock nudge her pussy. She pushed back, a silent demand. Liam laughed, sheathing himself in one long thrust.

Meredith cried out from the possession, stretched to her limit, widening her legs in a futile attempt to accommodate him. He moved in and out as her back arched, instinctively positioning herself so his head rubbed against her spot, again and again. He reached between their bodies and fingered her clit, rolling the swollen nub of flesh as her fucked her from behind, skin slapping against skin, growls escaping his throat even as high cries escaped hers. He tugged her hair, causing her back to arch.

"Liam, I can't take it," she cried out, desperate for relief. For a climax or just a break she wasn't certain. The pleasure intensified past the point she could handle the sensation. Her fingers clawed at the sheets as each thrust rammed her deep into the mattress.

"You can take it, you *will* take it. All of it."

He shifted his hips, grinding inside her. "Your pussy feels so good," he moaned. "Tight little slick hot pussy. Fuck. Mine. Mine to fuck, mine to taste. Mine."

Hands wrapped around her waist and she realized he'd been holding back before. With the extra grip he pounded into her. She rose on her hands, breasts bobbing in the air, the smack of his balls against her ass like thunder as the scent of sex permeated the air.

Meredith screamed, climax overcoming her in a wave of body blanketing relief. She felt her natural lubricant coat him, making him even slicker as he roared his release.

But he was still hard inside her. He pulled out, shooting cum onto her ass. She was pregnant; she didn't need his seed in her womb. He rubbed the cream in the crevice between her globes, smacking one cheek as his hands pulled apart her ass cheeks. The sting inflamed her; she wanted more. Wanted him to smack her ass until her skin burned. He rubbed more cum around her puckered entrance, Meredith trembling as a thick thumb pressed its way into her virgin hole.

"Liam," she said, voice shaky.

He caressed her ass then pulled away, weight leaving the bed. She looked over her shoulder, pushing hair away from her face as she watched him walk to his dresser and pull something out of the top drawer. When he turned back his face was no less savage, eyes no less full of sexual fury as he returned to the bed. She had to close her eyes or else lose her courage, her trust. His face was not the face of a man prepared to be gentle.

But when he covered her again his touch was light. "I won't hurt you," he said. "I'll go slowly, take my time. You still want to apologize, don't you, Meredith?"

She nodded, throat dry, saying nothing.

"Good."

Cool, slick fingers teased her entrance, thumb once more pushing inside her body. The sensation was strange, an invasion that felt both taboo and erotic.

"Relax," he murmured.

Meredith forced the tension to leave her body, giving herself completely to his dark possession. Abandoning trepidation, shyness, delving into the heart of her sensuality as a woman, a lover. She wanted everything he could give her; wanted him to take everything she had to give.

"Good girl."

Liam pushed in further, sliding past the tight ring of muscle. She felt her body clamp vise around his fingers, hugging the wide knuckles, the shape of his nail as his fingers moved inside her, an erotic tickling like the brush of fingers on the back of her hand or the inside of her thigh. Except more intense as she felt the spot inside her pussy pulse. The combined sensations brought a shiver of sound from her throat, a startled mewl. If she'd thought she was sated, drained, unable to feel anymore pleasure- she'd been wrong. Her body woke from its dazed slumber, clamoring for more.

He opened her further, taking time to continue to coat his fingers in the lubricant, taking his time to fuck her slowly, slowly, until her hips began to buck, demanding more of the almost painful pleasure.

"Liam, stop teasing me," she nearly growled, clit engorged and desperate for relief.

Her lover laughed. "This is *my* reward, not yours. But..."

He withdrew, and the next thing she knew the tip of his cock pressed against her hole, wet, silky, pressing in and in the channel he'd already prepared for his true possession. It was much different, accepting the size of his cock versus the size of his fingers, but once he was past muscle and inside, sheathed to balls that tickled the globes of her ass, he began to move.

Incredibly, it felt as good as if he were fingering her clit. The dual sensation when his fingers entered her pussy was almost too much to bear. Stretched taut, invaded, he fucked her with a growing strength, sliding in and out. She lowered herself onto her chest, ass in the air and reached between her legs to touch herself, rub the throbbing bit of flesh that offered, begged for her to taste ecstasy.

An orgasm built, trembling, preparing to throw her over the precipice. Her fingers moved faster, harder, matching the strokes of his hand, of his cock. Her mouth trembled open, as he rubbed her spot from inside her pussy and inside her ass, a relentless building pressure.

"Cum for me," he growled. "Now."

And she did, body exploding even as she felt the creamy heat of him inside of her ass, cum filling her as her juices coated his fingers. He roared, a primal sound of dark male satisfaction, having taken his woman for his pleasure and providing ecstasy in return. Branding her, binding her body and soul to him in the most primal way. Only Liam could make her body sing; she would never be able to touch another man again.

Meredith saw the missed call from Brick on her cell and hit return call.

"Brick?"

"Meredith?"

She sat up, disturbed by the girl's hushed tone. "Brick, what's wrong?"

"Can I come stay with you?"

"What? What's happened?"

"I just- I think my foster brother may be stalking me."

"But- he lives with you. Why would he- Brick, is he the reason your face was bruised the other week?"

She threw off the covers, cradling the cell between ear and shoulder. Pulling on sweats and slip on gym shoes, she pulled her hair back and left the bedroom, grabbing keys as she went.

"I'm on my way, just -"

"Meredith, where are you going?" Liam asked, appearing in the hall after she'd passed the kitchen.

"Brick's in trouble, I need to go get her," she replied brusquely, slamming the front door closed behind her.

The rumble of a growl warned her a split second before his hand wrapped around her upper arm. He grabbed her cell.

"Brick? This is Liam. What's wrong?"

"Give me back my cell!" Meredith jumped, swiping at his head.

He glanced at her, irritated, wrapping an arm around her middle and hauling her against his chest, immobile.

"Okay, but Meredith is pregnant. She can't come, I'll be there myself in a few minutes. Oof- Woman! Behave!"

"Then let me go," she said through gritted teeth.

He ended the call, lowering his head until his nose touched hers.

"Go back in the house. Sit down. Stay."

"You can't make me. No, Liam! She's my student, and she needs me. She's also my friend- I'm not sitting home while she may be in trouble."

He studied her face. "Fine, But you stay in the truck, you hear me?"

Meredith nodded, stiff. But figuring agreement was quicker than a fight.

They made fast time to Brick's house. The foster parents protested, but when Meredith growled at them, Liam backing her up with the threat of a call to the foster agency, their protests dried up.

Brick climbed into the SUV, a worn backpack slung over her shoulder.

"When we get home, you'll need to tell me everything Rebekah," Liam said. "We could get in trouble for taking you out of your placement- we need to have good cause to show. And we go to the police if it's warranted. Do you understand?"

The girl nodded jerkily, taking a deep breath. "I'll write everything down, too. I- I'm tough. But the next kid who comes to live with him might not be."

CHAPTER

15

"Meredith, can you come in here for a minute?"

She left the couch, putting aside her notes for the Teens and Greens winter program. Entering the kitchen, Liam sat at the island working on his laptop. It was a rare day for him to be home this time in the morning- lately he'd spent every last minute at the restaurant. He glanced up as she entered, expression impassive.

Her heart twisted, just a little. She knew she had to give him time to.... come to terms with everything that had happened. But she missed the easy warmth between them. Missed it, and wasn't sure how much longer she was willing to wait to get it back. Either he could be with her one hundred percent, or he could be without her. But this coolness- outside the bedroom, anyway- would have to stop.

"What is it?" she asked, leaning on her elbow next to him.

"I made an appointment in Seattle for this weekend. There's an OBGYN up there who specializes in high risk- and she's a Bear."

Meredith frowned at him. "Liam, you should have consulted me first. I wanted to pick my own doctor."

"Do you have medical insurance?" he asked, closing his laptop with a prissy finality that just... infuriated her.

He damn well knew she didn't have any kind of medical insurance. Private was too expensive, her work as a W-9 ESL instructor didn't come with any benefits, and she didn't qualify for state medical because she was a single, healthy woman. Though, she now realized, they'd probably cover her now since she was pregnant.

"No, I don't," she replied, relaxing her jaw. "But I can go to DHS in the morning-"

He laughed. "Funny."

"Well, how were you proposing I pay for this fancy obstetrician?" She held up a hand. "I understand you are well off-" she bit off the words "-but I am not. And I feel responsible to pay half of the medical costs- and I'm certain I can't afford even half of what a specialist in Seattle would charge an uninsured patient."

Liam rose, sliding the Mac under his arm. "I'm not arguing with you on this, Meredith."

"Then don't," she said to his back as he walked out. "Because I'm not going."

He stopped, turned. Meredith smiled at him, facing him fully and setting her feet. Liam studied her for a long moment, then shrugged a shoulder.

"Suit yourself," he said, leaving. "But if something goes wrong with the pregnancy- we both know who will be to blame."

That was it. "Now wait just one damn minute!" she yelled, striding after him.

He rounded on her as soon as she was within an inch of him. "Yes, sweetheart?"

Meredith bounded off his hard chest, grabbing his upper arm to keep from falling. He didn't budge an inch off balance.

"I'm getting a little tired of your attitude," she said, letting go of him. "I know we have issues between us-"

"You call lying to me an issue?"

She wanted to stomp, to jump around like a crazy woman and tear out her hair. Scream. She indulged the behavior in her head for a good minute until certain she could speak without looking psycho.

"If you can't get over that, then there is no point in us continuing."

"And what does that mean?" he asked softly.

She took a deep breath. "Look. I know you're a good man, Liam. You probably want to do the right thing by this baby. But-" she took a second to steady the tremble in her voice "-it seems as if the relationship just isn't what we both thought it would be. We aren't married, we haven't made any kind of commitment. Maybe it's time to- to walk away."

Each word was a tear in her heart. But she understood that if he couldn't forgive her and move on now, so early in their relationship, then there was little chance of them having a warm, loving family. She couldn't force him to love her, to want her outside of sex. She couldn't force him to respect her when he clearly thought of her as a deceiver.

And maybe she was. But she hadn't meant to hurt him and everyone made mistakes. It was time to either move on, whichever direction moving on meant.

"Are you done?" he asked, emotionless.

She stiffened. "Yes."

"We'll discuss this tonight when I come home."

"I might not be here."

His charcoal eyes paled to amber as the Bear peeked at her. "If you aren't here, I will hunt you down- and you won't like my mood when I catch you."

"He actually *said* that?" Tamar asked, aghast.

"He's an insensitive, Alpha pig jerk," Meredith said, pounding a fist on the bar. "I'm not one of his Bears! He treats me with an icicle chip on his shoulder all week, and then just arbitrarily picks my doctor and expects me to go along with it because he's rich and has a dick and then tells me, *tells me,* he'll hunt me down! Like a- a caveman! Why are you grinning, it's not funny!"

"It's kinda romantic, actually," Tamar said, leaning on the bar. She glanced at Alphonso, coming from the direction of the stockroom, sideways. "Shows he cares."

Meredith stared at her friend. "Are you out of your mind? It shows disrespect."

"What are you doing here?" Alphonso asked. He stopped next to

Tamar, ignoring her as he addressed Meredith. "You're pregnant. Get out."

Meredith gaped at him. "Has every Bear in this town lost their damn mind all of a sudden?"

"To many people in here smoke," he growled. "You don't need to be breathing that shit in. Get out. Go somewhere... girly. And don't come back in here until after you drop the cub. No, until after you wean the cub."

"You can't kick my best friend out," Tamar protested hotly.

He snorted. "My place. Just did."

Tamar whipped off her apron. "Then I quit."

Alphonso's eyes narrowed, attention shifting from Meredith to Tamar. "You can't quit," he replied, flat. "You have a cub to feed. You're a responsible mother, aren't you?"

Tamar's shoulders drooped a bit before her spine stiffened. "I'll get a *real* job. Come on, Meredith. Let's go."

"Oh, well... maybe you should stay," Meredith stammered. "I mean, he's right- quit if you want, but not until you have another job lined up."

Tamar stood, apron dangling, glaring at them both. "Maybe I don't want to work for someone else anymore. Maybe I want to actually use my fucking MBA and open my own business."

Alphonso crossed his arms. "That's what you want? Fine. You can manage my second location. And if you don't screw it up, we'll see about going halfsies."

"I- what? Halfsies? What?"

Meredith stifled a laugh, sliding off the stool, suddenly feeling much more cheerful. It was rare to see Tamar so... floored.

"Hey, I'll holla at you later, Tam. Looks like you got business to take care of."

She was pulling out of the gravel lot when Brick's ringtone went off. She clicked her Bluetooth.

"Brick?"

"Meredith," the girl's half growl, half high pitched shaky sound of panic alerted her.

"Brick, what's wrong?"

"At the Y, hurry. Harvey's been stabbed."

"*What?*"

"Hurry hurry, damn."

Meredith clamped down on her spurt of panic, forcing herself to drive steady. It wouldn't help if she got in an accident. "Brick, calm down."

"I'm calm." The girl's razor sharp tone flayed Meredith.

"Are you safe?"

"For now."

"I need you to hang up and call 911. I'm on my way. Harvey is blood type A+, okay?"

"Alright. Hurry."

Meredith glanced both ways as she came up to the next stop sign, and floored it.

She beat the ambulance, probably because she was already on the way. Meredith screeched into the parking lot, engine jerking as she ripped out the key at the same time she put it in park. Cursing because she hadn't bothered to ask Brick where she was, she looked around wildly, heart racing.

"Meredith, over here!" Bricks hoarse shout alerted her.

She ran to the garden, skidding to a stop behind the shed. "Go watch for the ambulance, I've got him," she said, forcing calm into her voice as she dropped to her knees.

Harvey was gray, lying in a pool of blood. Meredith saw, and approved, the strips of flannel wrapped around the site of the injury. Glancing at the teenager, she realized Brick was clad only in her usual cargoes and a thin tank, oversized flannel gone- used to make a field bandage. Sirens sounded in the background. She took her father's hand as his eyes opened, dazed.

"Dad, the ambulance is here, it will be okay."

"Meredith," he whispered. "Baby girl. Sorry."

"Don't talk, Dad. Brick, what happened?" she asked when the girl returned with paramedics who shooed the two women out of the way.

"It was Ron," Brick said, hoarse, wrapping slender arms around her middle.

"Ron?"

"My foster brother. He was aiming for me. Harvey stepped in the way."

"Oh my God," Meredith said, face white. The paramedics lifted Harvey onto a stretcher. "Can I ride with him? I'm his daughter. And my student as well, she's a witness to the attack."

One of them glanced at her, nodding. "The police will want to talk to both of you."

They walked briskly to the nearby ambulance, climbing into the back. The paramedics worked rapidly, voices a soothing monotone. They were doing everything they could do for him. He would make it.

At the hospital they wheeled Harvey straight into emergency surgery, leaving the two women behind in the waiting room. Meredith clutched Brick's hand.

"He'll be alright. We got here in time."

She kept saying it, hoping her words would make it true.

"Ma'am?"

Meredith glanced at the officer who approached her, controlling the instinctive shrink because he was a tall, blond male with wide shoulders. Military training from the cut of his hair and the way he held himself.

"Yes?"

"I have a few questions to ask you."

She nodded. "That's fine but my student Brick was the one who witnessed everything- I arrived after she called me."

He nodded, pulling out a pad. "Let's start at the beginning."

Brick gave her report, telling of how her foster brother Ron had tracked her to the garden. They'd argued and he'd pulled a knife.

"What was the argument about?" the officer interrupted, looking skeptical.

Brick said nothing. The officer's eyes narrowed. "Young lady, this is a very serious matter."

The girl muttered something, looking down. Meredith touched her shoulder.

"Brick, what is it?" she asked.

"No one will believe me."

"I believe you."

The teenager shrugged, jerky. "He's been trying to get me to sleep with him. Says since his parents feed me, I owe him. But he's this darling at school-good grades and popular. I'm just the troubled foster kid."

"I see," the officer said, expression grave. "Is this the first time he's approached you for sex?"

"No. I told him if he ever managed to rape me, he'd better make sure I was dead because I wouldn't stop coming after him."

The girl continued her story, telling of how Ron cornered her, pulled a knife after a verbal altercation, how Brick had screamed for help. Harvey appeared out of nowhere and wrestled with the boy, who managed to stab him and then ran.

"Did he have the weapon when he ran?"

Brick's eyes narrowed. "No, man. I think- I almost think he dropped it. I glanced at him to make sure he was leaving while I was helping Harvey and I don't remember seeing anything in his hands. He must have dropped it in the garden."

Meredith shook her head. Stupid. But she felt grimly satisfied. That knife would be the evidence they needed to put the boy away.

"Alright." The office pulled out his radio and called the squad car on the scene, relaying the data. Then the officer turned to Meredith, expression shifting slightly.

"You said your name is Meredith Tyler- you're Liam's woman, aren't you?"

Meredith stared at him, taken aback. "Um... we're... dating."

"Does he know you're here?" The officer shook his head, seeing the expression on her face. She remembered Liam's words about tracking her down.

"Yeah," the cop said. "I think you should call him, let him know. Might piss him off to hear about this from someone else, you know?"

"How do you know Liam?" she asked.

"How do you think?"

Meredith realized, then, that the officer must be a Bear, and a member of Liam's... Den.

"Thanks, Officer," she said. "I'll call him." Only she didn't.

CHAPTER

1 6

Fury threatened rational thought. She wasn't here. He'd been so certain she would be waiting for him. Over the weeks together he'd become certain she must love him, must want a life with him. Meredith wasn't a woman who indulged in casual affairs, formed commitments to people without coming to care for them. He'd held off biting her, making her his mate because he wanted her to have time. A Mating was permanent. Once he bit her, he could never let her go. So she had to be sure.

His first instinct was to track her down and shake her. The second instinct was to let her go- he couldn't keep a woman who didn't want to be kept. What shocked him the most was his sense of loss, almost... grief. He'd wanted her to stay with him of her own free will. Wanted a family with her. And she'd left him.

Liam realized he'd behaved badly that week. He'd been telling himself that he just needed a time to reconcile his past with his present, with his future. But now time was up. But damn her if she thought he was going to let her walk away because she couldn't deal with him when he was feeling a bit growly. Liam pulled out his cell just as it rang, about the decline the call impatiently, then changed his mind.

"Conroy."

"Alpha? This is Officer Bret Anders."

"Bret?" Liam frowned. He knew Bret, though they'd never been more than acquaintances. He was a valuable member of the Den and one of Liam's ears in the local police force. Bret was able to ensure incidences involving Bears were quietly referred to Liam and never reported. The Clans didn't quite have legal sovereignty, but there was an unspoken understanding with local government agencies. As long as the Alpha's did their jobs.

"Meredith is at the hospital."

His heart stopped, breath sucked from his chest. "What? "He was calm only because he didn't have the power in his lungs to roar. Meredith. The cub.

"She's fine. She wasn't the victim, just a witness."

"What the fuck is going on?" he growled, already striding out of the door.

"We only have a preliminary report, but it appears her father was nearly stabbed to death while defending a teenage girl from an assailant. One of the students."

"I'm on my way."

The doctor came out of surgery several hours later. Meredith was still up on fumes alone- and coffee, though she supposed she shouldn't be guzzling it the way she was.

"He almost didn't make it," the doctor said. "A few more minutes would have done him in. He lost a lot of blood, but we were able to repair the internal lacerations. I'd suggest you go home and get some rest, there isn't anything else you can do. We'll call you when he wakes up."

Meredith shook her head. "I want to stay until he wakes up."

"Meredith."

Her head whipped around at the sound of Liam's deep voice. She forgot her anger, her trepidation, and ran to him. His arms swept her into a tight hug, cradling her against his body.

"It's alright, baby," he murmured. "This is my fault. I'm so sorry."

"How is it your fault?" she cried, looking up at him.

He grimaced. "Should have killed the punk when I started to."

"Liam- you can't just-"

He shook his head. "I know, forget I said anything." But he glanced over her shoulder at the Bear Officer, who'd reappeared in the room.

Meredith realized who must have called her lover, but couldn't feel resentment. She was too tired for resentment.

On the heels of that thought her knees began to tremble. "I think I need to sit down."

Liam lifted her, settling on a nearby bench with her in his lap. "Brick?" he called, voice deep with her ear against his chest. "Are you okay? Is there someone you need to call?"

"Who am I going to call?" the teenager asked flatly. "The social worker will probably put me in a group home until they place me again."

Liam was silent a moment. Meredith struggled to keep her eyes open. She was exhausted all of a sudden, the caffeine she'd been running on leaving her until there was nothing but mushy marrow in place of bones.

"I'll talk to the social worker," she heard him say. "You'll come home with us."

"Really?"

"Yeah. You'll have to earn your keep though- that my garden in the backyard is in a sad, sad state."

"No problem, I can do that."

Meredith smiled, hearing the deliberate nonchalance in her student's voice. It exactly matched the nonchalance in Liam's. They were both big teddy Bears, all bark and no bite. And on the heels of that thought she allowed her mind to drift and her body to go limp.

She woke briefly as he put her into the SUV, and again when he tucked her into bed. The next morning she didn't wake up until well past the time of her first class. Recalled with a smile that in the past, whenever she read in a romance novel that the hero put the girl to bed without her waking up, it sounded silly. Glancing at her cell, she saw several missed calls and cursed, though halfheartedly, and only because Liam's language was a bad influence. When she explained the events of the previous evening, her company would understand.

Meredith decided to shower and put on fresh clothing before going downstairs. Whatever issues she and Liam needed to deal with- she wanted to be clean. But when she emerged from the bathroom, soaped and lotioned, hair damp, he was sitting on the bed, waiting.

She stopped short, staring at him. "Are you mad?" she asked.

His brow rose. "Why would I be mad?"

"You said-"

Air blew out of flared nostrils. "I think, under the circumstances, Meredith," he said, voice hot and dry, "there isn't much room for anger."

"Did the hospital call?"

"Yes. He woke up this morning. No, don't go anywhere. He needs to rest. They said to come on by this evening, he should wake back up on his own then."

She nodded, hesitating. Liam sighed. "Come here, baby."

Meredith walked into the outstretched arms. He settled her on his lap, echoing the previous evening, lips brushing the top of her head

"I'm sorry, Meredith."

"What for?"

"I've been an ass." He paused. "What your Dad did for Brick- a girl he doesn't even really know- he isn't the same person."

"No, he's not." She'd seen that over the last few weeks.

"I can't promise to be happy about it, but I can try to forgive him. A little bit at a time."

"Okay."

She turned her head towards him, seeking his lips with her own, capturing him in a soft kiss, hands going to his shoulders. His arms tightened around her as he deepened the kiss, tongue sliding in between her lips, fingers biting into her waist.

"Are we okay?" she asked after a minute, pulling back. "It occurred to me

337

that we have been going pretty fast. I know it must be a shock to suddenly become a father. I want this to work out, and I'm willing to-"

"Shut up." He kissed her again, this time eschewing gentleness for pure male passion. "You aren't going anywhere. I'm not going anywhere."

He stood, lifting her enough to toss her gently onto the bed, immediately covering her body with his own. "Don't you understand anything yet? You're mine, Meredith. I'm not letting you go. Ever."

"Then-" she licked her lips. "Does that mean we're still dating?"

He laughed at her, dark and humorless. "Sweetheart, we are so not dating." Dark eyes paled to amber eyes her. "Humans and their... paltry... notions. Dating."

Shaking his head, he ripped the towel from her body, head lowering to nuzzle her breasts. She gasped as his mouth closed over her nipple. Hands roving over his chest after he took a moment to remove his clothing.

"Then- if we aren't- *Liam*- dating, then what are we doing?"

Fingers plunged into her already slick pussy, playing with her, coaxing a moan from her throat.

"Right now? We're going to fuck. And while my cock is in you, I'm going to bite you. And you'll be my mate. My woman. Forever."

Those words strummed a chord of longing she'd buried so deep in her heat it pained her to acknowledge it now. It would be so easy to fall into the sexual haze, but...

"Do you love me, Liam?" she asked. He stilled, looking down at her.

She plunged on. "Your mother told me why you started courting me in the first place. I know lots of people make marriages work where there is no love, but- that's not what I want for myself."

"What's love, Meredith?"

She refused to look down, refused to allow the soft tone to divert her from this one truth she needed to move forward. "Why don't you tell me?"

"Love is forgiveness, sometimes for the sake of another person. Love is responsibility, when you create life together." His hand cupped her mound. "Love is passion." Head lowering, his lips brushed hers once, twice, then trailed over her cheek and down her neck. "Love is also time, Meredith. And I want to spend the rest of my time with you. So yes, I love you."

She took a deep breath, blinking. "Okay." Her hands delved into his hair, drawing his face up so she could look into his eyes. "Okay. I love you, too, you know."

He smiled, arrogance peeking through the softness. "I know that, Meredith."

Her eyes widened and she released his hair to smack him. Liam laughed, knee nudging apart her thighs, eyes trained on hers, watching as her expression flickered, emptied of thought as he slid into her, filling her. Loving her, the pace he set slow and languorous. Pleasure built even as the scent of him, of them, filled her lungs. Wrapping her legs around his waist, she closed her eyes, losing herself in the feel of his cock inside her. It overwhelmed her, a rush of feeling, the sudden snap of a connection that felt... other. A contented, heated rumble in her head, like and unlike Liam's voice. Demanding she acknowledge its presence. Her eyes snapped open and she cried out, climax overwhelming her just as Liam lowered his head to her neck, nuzzling the hollow above her collarbone.

And bit down.

Meredith lay in the bed propped on a pile of thick pillows, wondering why everyone else was acting like she should be exhausted.

"I just gave birth," she said to Liam. "I didn't almost die."

He looked up from the infant in his arms, eyes flashing. "You have no idea how that looked from my end."

Meredith snort-giggled, then laughed. Trying to stifle the noise so she wouldn't wake the poor baby.

Gwenafar entered the bedroom, a tray in her hand. "Your mother went to grab the tea bags for your swelling, dear. She left her purse when you called. I told her first babies don't come that quickly. I suppose I was wrong."

Liam laughed. He could, now that it was over. Meredith smiled as well. The home birth went shockingly fast- probably because Meredith spent several hours in what she hadn't realized was early labor, thinking she was just overdoing the gardening work. Which she'd been deliberately overdoing in an attempt to get the baby, at forty-two and one half weeks, to come out already.

Meredith reached for the little girl. "She's the perfect size, too." She stared at the infants sleeping face, ran a finger gently through thick black hair.

Her mother in law sat on the bed. "I told you she wasn't overdue. I don't care what that doctor said. Natural gestation is longer than forty weeks for first time mothers. If you just let nature runs its course-"

"Okay, Ma," Liam said. "You should be a midwife."

Gwenafar sniffed. "I think I will. No one is too old to discover a new passion."

Meredith ate bites of a sandwich her husband and mate fed her while the baby nursed. Dozed until a flood of happy astonishment warmed the Den connection she shared with Liam's Bears through their mate bond.

Opening her eyes, she saw him set aside his cell, looking guilty. She smiled. "Group text?"

He kissed her. "I couldn't wait any longer. One more text asking me if the cub is here yet..."

Meredith leaned her head back on his shoulder. "We have to get Boden married. He's driving me crazy."

"One problem at a time, baby. He'll be next."

OTHER TITLES

Alphonso's Baby

Norelle's Bear

Bear Prince

Bear Princess

Warrior's Bond

Fae Spark